SiliCon

PRATIK UMESH VYAS

[Research by SNEHASHISH MISHRA]

Contents

Prologue

It is a scorching sunny day in Delhi in 2005 and Taksh is standing on the footpath of a parking space, dressed in formal attire with worn out slippers; Taksh is an average built mid-heighted young lad in his early 20s, with very boy next door kind of physical features — medium broad nose, a moderately defined jawline and an innocent smile. Taksh is holding a zip file bag which he keeps on the seat of a bike parked beside him. Then, Taksh continuously dials a number, puts the phone to his ears and disconnects at the 1st or 2nd ring.

A man in a funky orange cap, black sunglasses on his forehead and leather jacket, twirling keys on his finger walks from behind Taksh and stops by the bike, he sees a file resting on the pillion seat, he picks it up and flings it off. Taksh turns back and stares at the guy, but doesn't utter a word, it was one of his unlikely qualities, he barely took a stand for himself. Taksh picks up the file and rubs off the dust.

The guy adjusts his underwear from over the pants and sits on the bike, put his arm into the helmet slides it up till his elbows, looks at Taksh, bangs his head making the sunglass fall from the forehead and drops on his nose perfectly covering his eyes, he throttles the bike in neutral unnecessarily, then puts it into gear and rides off.

Taksh's phone rings, he picks up it in a jiffy. The man on the other side frowns at Taksh, "*Pagla gaya hai kya saale? Itna miss call kaun marta hai?*"

"*Bhai talktime bhar de mummy ka...bar bar mujhe miss call de rahi hai.. main jaldi jaldi mein bhul gaya..*"
Taksh pleads.

"*Jaa nahi karra.. rakh phone.*" The other person hangs up.

Taksh looks at the screen and smiles as the call gets disconnected for he knew in a matter of minutes, the recharge would be done. As he looks around, he see Harman, his friend and colleague who gave up his job to work with Taksh in his dream project. Imran is walking behind Harman with a blazer bag, Imran is Taksh's college senior who has always stood beside him like a pillar. Imran has seen a certain kind of spark in Taksh that once he carried but couldn't channelize it due to family pressure.

Harman and Imran ask Taksh to stretch his hands as they put the coat upon him. *"Fits? "* Harman raises his brows, Taksh nodes in head.

"Kitne pade sir iske?" Taksh asks Imran.

"You need not to worry about it. I've bought it for you," Imran says.

"No sir. Aap kyun karoge? Aap please mujhe bataiye kitne ka pada ye?". Taksh gets uncomfortable and is taking is wallet out from his pocket.

Imran stops him and says, *"bas..ho gaya.. kabhi toh kisiko kuch toh karne diya kar.. abhi bas jis kaam ke liye aya hai wahan dhyaan se.. sab ho jayega toh main tujhse khud maang lunga jo mujhe chahiye.."*

"Enough boys! Bas bas hogaya... tu nikal ab.. " Imran asks him to go and all three of them turn to the secretariat building and stare with admiration. Taksh calms himself down as he is walking towards the entrance, his phone chimes with his mother's call again.

Taksh opens the message and looks around, a lot of people were eyeing at him, he feels a little conscious but ignores everyone and but his mother calls again

"Hello Maa.." Taksh utters as he picks up.*"Hello! Haan Tukku..bol..*

tu thik hai.. nashta kiya?"

"Haan ma.. papa thik hai?"

Pramila looks at her husband lying beside her on the bed as she has the phone squeezed between her shoulder and ears, she is also peeling off garlic as she talks to Taksh on the phone.

"Maa.. main abhi Pradhan Mantri ke office mein hoon.. Papa... Papa sun rahe hai kya?" Taksh asks about his father.

The phone was on speaker, his father hears him and turns his face to the other.

"haan sun rahe hai.. tu bol... Tune kuch khaya hai?"

"Baad mein baat karta hoon maa!" Taksh hangs up.

"Accha apna khayal rakhna.. kuch khaa len—" Pramila realises the call is disconnected. He then, calls his girlfriend, Isha but the call goes unanswered.

Taksh immediately rectifies his mistake and now becomes more conscious, he held his file tightly when he suddenly unzipped the file bag, took out his pen and put it in his coat's pocket. He looks around with a little more confidence and a wider smile.

As Taksh ambles to the enquiry desk through the long lobby, armed guards are standing on both the sides, ministers, secretaries, other high ranking officials, police force and NSG is seen marshalling all around. Taksh clears his throat as he reaches the desk.

"Yes?" the receptionist asks.

"I've an appointment with Prime Minister sir", Taksh reveals.

"Yes you must be Mr Taksh Dabral.." receptionist confirms.

"Yes! I am."

"Please make yourself comfortable and wait for a while. PM sir is in a meeting." She shows him the seating area.

There were three sofas kept in a U shape with a dedicated tea table before each of them. There were magazines, newspapers and water bottles. Taksh takes a seat on the corner of a sofa, a peon comes and asks him for tea or coffee. Taksh gently denies, he is all nervous, tapping his feet, biting his nails occasionally when Sanath comes from behind and taps his shoulder. Taksh turns back hurriedly.

"Relax.. chai lelo.. it is nice here." Sanath gestures to the peon to get a cup of tea. "Enjoy your tea and wait... I'll go and check some other things," Sanath walks to the reception, talks a little with the receptionist and walks away.

He sees Sanath standing at the door of the PM cabin and waving his hand, gesturing to Taksh to join him, the receptionist also reminds him to go. Taksh stands, buttons his coat and marches to the PM cabin.

"Ready?" Sanath holds his shoulders.

"Hmm.." Taksh nods and both walk into the PM cabin, as they approach in, the door closes from behind.

❧❧❧

"Aaj toh baat kar lete... apka hi toh sapna pura karne gaya hai.." Pramila tells Samrish as she continues to peel garlic cloves.

"Mere sapno ne 7 saal pehle hi khud khushi kar li thi.. ye uski zid

hai.. mere sapno ko dhaal bana ke woh bas apni zid puri karna chahta hai.." Samrish puts his leg on his other leg. Pramila gets up with the peeled garlic and walks out of the bedroom. Samrish closes his eyes, no sooner did he do that, auditory hallucinations and flashbacks began flashing before his closed eyes — sounds of firing, sounds of mortar fired, tanks in action, explosives, grenades, and visuals of soldiers lying dead on the battlefield covered in dust and blood all mixed together, some of them with torn off limbs, severely burnt, shot at heads, popped out eyes.

Samrish immediately opens his eyes, looks around, is about to call Pramila but doesn't; sighs and closes his eyes again as he rests his half-folded pillow. It was one of things, he had a specific pillow that he would fold in half before resting his head on.

1962:

It's the same secretariat building, same corridor, less guards and a few Britishers striding around the corridor, a receptionist is answering calls on the telephone, the PM cabin has two guards with rifles on either sides of the door. The PRIME MINISTER sign board on the door is carved on a wooden plate with a wooden frame. The letters are in gold, the frame is in black. Two Indiangentlemen — Tungabhadra Rakshit and Lokbhushan Dabral are in three piece suits and are sitting on the sofa with a kid of 10 or 11, the sofas are as trendy as they could be for that time. There were a few glasses and a jug full of water on the centre of the tea table. There were newspapers scattered on the table. The front pages of all of those newspapers had black and white pictures of corpses of soldiers martyred in the battlefield; some with bullet wounds on forehead, some with their bodies burnt and covered in blood, the kid was staring at those pictures without a blink. Lokbhushan noticed it and distracted the kid while he folded the newspapers covering the front pages.

The kid leaned on the sofa, swinging his legs, swirling the thread of his lattu around his index finger. Rakshit and Dabral were looking at the closed door of the PM cabin with hopeful eyes. They both look at each other and then look back at the door. The door opens, and 4 Whitemen walk out of the door with disappointed faces, discussing something among themselves. Rakshit and Dabral rush towards them along with the kid and begin inquiring about things. Dabral asks, "Is anything wrong?"

One of the white men sigh, "EVERYTHING." He pats Dabral's shoulders and continues, "Dabral, INDIA is yet to be ready for this venture between FAIRKID CORP. and you people. I don't think we can come to a mutual agreement with the current government and their policies."

Dabral and Rakshit look at each other with lowered faces. As the Fairkid people walk out, one of them turns and looks at the confused faces of both the Indians and offers a job to Dabral and Rakshit at FAIRKID Malaysia office. He asks them to give it a thought and revert back. Rakshit and Dabral keep looking cluelessly at the white men as they walk out of the lobby.

Dabral frowns and marches to the PM cabin forcefully trying to enter but the guards hold him back, one of the staff from inside comes out. Dabral commands them to let him meet the prime minister but the staff calmly asks him not to behave that way and informs that the PM is leaving for Srinagar as the condition at the borders is worsening. Dabral and Rakshit may take an appointment for next week. Dabral was adamant to go inside right then but he failed. Dabral strolls out of the lobby, Rakshit calls out to the kid, "Samrish" who was staring at his father walking away. Rakshit along with Samrish followed Dabral out of the office.

About The Author

Pratik Umesh Vyas is a dynamic force in the creative industry, serving as the Founder and Managing Director of VirgiNotions, a film and web production company known for its innovative storytelling. With a degree in Film Direction and Production Management from the prestigious London School of Film & Television, Pratik brings over seven years of rich experience in filmmaking and television, both in India and internationally. His expertise lies in direction, story development, and screenplay writing, allowing him to craft compelling narratives that resonate with audiences.

Now, he expands his creative horizons by debuting as an author with his captivating book, 'Silicon.' This intriguing work of fiction delves into India's struggles with the semiconductor industry, weaving together factual data, real-life incidents, and authentic timelines to create a thought-provoking narrative. Pratik's ability to blend fiction with reality not only entertains but also enlightens readers, making him a prominent voice in contemporary storytelling.

"Storytelling is the bridge that connects cultures and hearts."

Note To The Reader

You may have read dozens of stories about successes and about victories that are carved on the pages of history as prepossessing and as prominent as supernovas in the known and unknown omniverses. Unlike anything like that, this story covers the historical timeline from Cholera to Corona. This story is about a thirsty lost nomad in a desert who is bamboozled throughout with a mirage of a lake and keeps tramping towards the lake of mirage until he is perished into nothingness of the desert sand and his existence is erased by erosions through eternities. This story is about a failure, a failure that was followed by another failure and then further followed by another failure and finally finishes with one more failure until the HERO of the story decides to move a chair and the timeline of failures shatter down like dust and debris.

CHAPTER ONE

Basic Beginnings

BACK TO 2005:

The meeting was supposed to be with the PM but it was somebody else, an ex minister of MeitY [MINISTRY OF ELECTRONICS AND INFORMATION TECHNOLOGY] but the meeting went better than Taksh's expectations. But throughout the meeting Taksh was asked about his father's patent files of a semicon chip technology that only his father was able to crack years back. The minister and Sanath advised him to get it from his father else it won't be possible to make the ground breaking technology a reality. Taksh assured them, he'll get the required papers and submit them to the ministry at the earliest. Taksh is assured that the orders for the list of machinery required will be processed that same day and Taksh will officially lead the entire venture. At the end of the meeting, Taksh is reminded to get the technology patent from his father as Samrish successfully developed 0.8 micron chips whereas Taksh was still perfecting his 2.2 micron chip and 2.2 chips were not a groundbreaking technological discovery, China, South Korea, Japan were already doing it.

Taksh explains them that he would be able to achieve 0.8 or at least 1 micron tech but Sanath tells him not put extra effort when he can inherit it from Samrish.

As Taksh walks out of the cabin with a gleeful face, we see Sanath walking along him telling him a lot of things.

"Jaise hi cargo pounchta hai... hum batate hai..tum apne papa se patent ke papers le lena unki zarurat padegi.." Sanath taps his back. Taksh nods his head.

"Land details aur capital requirements ki file toh do warna pass kaise karwaunga funding?" Sanath reminds him, Taksh hands him the file. Sanath reminds him again to submit the patent papers as soon as it was possible.

Taksh is in an auto, he dials some numbers makes a call to Rao — UDYAN RAO who is like a mentor to Taksh. Udyan Rao worked in the ISRO and came from a family of landlords. Taksh and Rao met for the first time during an inter school science fair and since then, Rao was fond of Taksh and has supported him by all means. Rao was the one who connected Taksh with Sanath and made the deal possible with the government. The government had approved the projects a number of times in the past few decades but this was the first time, Government took an action and was about to purchase the machinery for the set up of the semiconductor plant.

The ring continues for half a minute before Rao answers the call.

"Boliye Dabral Sahab..." he chuckles.

"Sir.." Taksh keeps shush.

"Mohali kab tak lautiyega?" Rao breaks the ice for him.

"Bas bus adde hi pounch raha hoon raat ki bus hai.. kal subah tak laut jaunga.." Taksh answers.

"Chaliye fir toh.. ek baar abhi shaam tak aiye bus lene se pehle..." Rao

invites him home.

"Aaj nahi Uncle! Ab thoda maa papa ke saath baithunga aur waise bhi itne din baad gaya toh aaj toh maa waise bhi nikalne nahi degi.. 2 4 din mein milu wapas Delhi aake?" Taksh excuses.

Rao lets out a breath and bellowed on the phone, *"Karamkaant! Raat mein kya banana hai Isha se puch lena.."* he paused for a second and continues, *"Chaliye thikhai fir.. jab mann ho ajana.. hum toh bekar log hai.. ab toh aapke rishte seedhe pradhan mantri se hai aap toh busy hone waale hai. —"*

"Nahi, Uncle." Taksh cuts his words midway, *"nahi nahi...mujhe yaad aya woh dono kahin jaa rahe hai... main ajaun kya fir shaamko?"* he puts up a fake laughs as he says this.

"PAKKA?" Rao confirms.

"Haan Uncle..waise Isha wapas agayi hai?" Taksh asks hesitantly.

"HAAN.. kal shaam ko hi agayi thi.. chalo ab dabral saab aap jaiye... gharwaalo ko time dijiye.. jab free ho jaye toh bataiyega.. rakhte hai.."

"Thikhai uncle... Main ataa hoon.."

Rao laughs on the phone and disconnects.

Pramila and Samrish are in an autorickshaw, the sun is blazing in the sky, the hot wind is blasting on their faces as auto rickshaw slides through the empty roads.

"Tukku shaam ko araha hai.. aaj kam se kam thik se baat kijiyega usse." Pramila requests Samrish.

"*Kya hua plan pass hua uska..*" Samrish asks. Then answers himself, "*Main bata raha hoon usko sab bewakoof bana rahe hai usko... Kuch nahi hoga..*"

"*arre seedhe pradhan mantri ne haan kara hai.*" Pramila utters with a pinch of pride in her voice.

Samrish turns his face the other way and looks outside, his eyes tear up and due to the winds, the teardrops roll down his temples and stretch up to his cheeks. Samrish was always against Taksh's decision of following the footsteps of his grandfather and father. Samrish has lost more than he ever gained from the constant tussle of a lifetime. He always believed the government and society did wrong to him. He deserved better.

Soon after, the autorickshaw stopped, "*bhaiya thoda sa araam se..*" Pramila expressed distress. They were at the gate of the hospital. Pramila and Samrish hop down from the autorickshaw, Pramila asked for the fare and then had a little of a bargain battle with the autowala. Followed by the battle they walk inside, talk for the appointment at the reception and sit on a bench beside the reception desk.

"*Sarkari haspatal mein bhi toh ho hi jata.. faltu mein paiso ka shrraadh karne yahan agayi..*" Samrish mutters; Pramila shushes him.

Samrish was to be taken into the MRI room, a wardboy comes with a wheelchair. Samrish glares at him and frowns, "*Abhi tak zarurat nahi padi hai iski.. chalne layak hoon main..*" gets up and begins walking.

"*Oh! Tau.. Idharr..*" the wardboy calls out, Samrish turns back and starts following him.

Samrish follows the wardboy into the MRI room and lays down on the MRI bed, the wardboy belts him properly, he slides into the machine, a voice from outside advises Samrish to keep his closed and not open until further command. Samrish takes a deep breath and closes his eyes.

1962:

An adolescent Samrish is walking to the help desk of the PMO along with Lokbhushan and Tungabhadra. As the lady at the help desk saw them approaching she offered them a seat and whispered something to one of the staff who then rushed to the guard standing at the gate of the PM cabin. The guard then knocks and enters inside. He comes out after a few minutes. Dabral and Rakshit are gestured to follow the staff but as they walk towards the PM cabin, they are stopped and shown another way. Confused, both walk behind the staff who walks them inside a cabin which had no board on the gate. A man in his 50s or late 40s was resting on the chair, he greets them and offers them a seat. He looks at the staff asking him to take the child out for sometime but Samrish wraps himself around his father and after a few failed attempts Dabral requests to let him be as he won't interrupt the meeting in any possible way. Samrish sat down on a sofa quite far away from the desk and began sketching something in his sketchbook.

Rakshit politely asks the man about his role in the entire scenario as the appointment was with the PM himself. The man didn't reveal his identity and looked at them for a second with glaring eyes, then spoke, *"Do you think the PM is so jobless he will have to address the issue of a random transistor company?"*

Dabral and Rakshit stared at the man with annoyance. The man continued, *"besides, he isn't available right now, he is yet to return from Srinagar."*

What else could you expect from the leaders of a nation that got independence just a decade ago, directionless and restless.. the government barely knew the right and wrong or how their decisions were going to shape the nation's future.

Dabral and Rakshit blinklessly stare at him without a word. The man continued further as he sighed, *"See, currently we are not interested in making radios and transistors we need weapons for defence."*

"It is just not for radios, in the future your weapons will require it as well." Dabral defended.

"In the future right?" He plonks his hands on the table. *"So when the future comes we will consider your plan but for now it is not required, we can't be wasting our national treasure upon something like this. We need to watch our expenses as the ammunition we import is not free. India is not strong enough to think of anything else but its freedom. It has hardly been a decade since we have tasted freedom. Do you want to be slaves again?"*

The man calms himself and speaks further, *"See we were really okay with it but those Americans were not okay with complying with our policies and without that we cannot let them enter India and give them the access to our land."*

"But they are just interested in the business." Rakshit interrupted.

"Yeah! Similarly, with similar excuses, the Britishers came to India a few centuries back and the rest is known to all so do you really want to trust these Whitemen again?"

"The world is changing, it is not what you think it is, the world is evolving." Dabral explains.

"You are delusional, nothing has changed and nothing will. There are

dozens of other countries still fighting for freedom, still under European colonisation. It is a matter of just one opportunity and India will be engulfed by these colonisers again. Besides, India is currently in an ongoing war with China and we are currently focused on it."

"India needs growth and semiconductor chips are the way to achieve it." Rakshit tries to convince him again.

"What India currently needs is his soldiers and ammunition to protect itself against the Chinese and not some radio." The man raises his voice now.

"You are running a country so big and yet you are so ignorant about the future.. a country like Pakistan which is not even one-fourth of our size and didn't even receive half of the resources we have.. and it got its independence on the same day as we did and yet they are developing, manufacturing their own weapons, and you know what's a matter of more shame to you and your entire government? Pakistan recently inaugurated its own space program too and India doesn't even have one." Lokbhushan taunted him.

"Enough, we have to save our land first, then wonder about the sun, moon and stars. Anyway, let's call it a day. If, in the future your idea is relevant, the government will surely give it a thought but for now, It's useless." The man folds his hands and asks them to leave.

Disappointed, distressed, disturbed, dissatisfied, dismayed, discouraged, dispirited, disgruntled, both of them walk out. Dabral walked a little ahead of Rakshit, Samrish saw them walking out and ran to them, Rakshit called him and accompanied him out of the place, walking a few steps behind Dabral.

PRESENT DAY:

The bed slides out of the MRI scanner, Samrish opens his eyes. Samrish walks out of the MRI room and finds Pramila waiting. They both stroll out from the main gate of the hospital. They saw the same auto rickshaw they came to the hospital in. The autorickshaw driver asks them to drop them back. *"Rukne ka koi alag se paisa nahi dungi,"* Pramila clarified.

"Arre chachi... baithiye na.. maanga kya apse?"

"Pehle se saaf bol dena chahiye." Pramila hops inside after Samrish.

Pramila and Samrish reach home. The house was at a walking distance of 50m from the main road in a narrow lane wide enough for two wheelers and three wheelers only. Their house had 3 bedrooms, two on the left and one on the right, beside the right bedroom was the toilet and the kitchen and the right one was Taksh's.

The hall was a basic hall with an armless sofa by a wall, a small television, few speakers and above that wall was a hanging mandir which was Pramila's favourite spot. The kitchen door didn't have a door but had a curtain over it and so did all other doors in the house. Samrish sits on his rocking chair that once belonged to Rakshit and before him Lokbhushan used it. Pramila strips out the tablet and passes it to Samrish, Samrish gulps the medicine down with a sip of water. Pramila tucks him in the bed, just then the power goes off. Samrish smirks, *"Iss desh mein logo ko dene ke loye toh bijlee hai nahi... factory aur industry kahan se lagayenge.... pata nahi kya hi hoga?"*

Pramila stays quiet as she knows that the power was out because the bill was unpaid. She goes to the kitchen and miss-calls her son a number of times. Taksh calls her back. *"Hello! Haan maa!"*

"Awaaz arahi hai?" Pramila confirms.

"Haan maa.."

"Woh test karne mein aur saare paise khatam hogaye. Woh bijlee ke bill ke bhi. Dawai waale pe bhi udhari badh gayi hai."

"Koi baat nahi ab toh meri naukri hai aur paise hi paise aane waale hai.. main kal tak karta hoon kuch...bhar dunga bill", Taksh consoles her. The family was going through extreme financial constraints since all their savings was to be put for Samrish's illness.

"Hmm.. tune kuch khaya?" Pramila asks her son.

"Maa.. rakhta hoon balance khatam ho raha hai...aake baat karta hoon." Taksh disconnects the call.

Pramila goes back to the bedroom while Samrish was sleeping, she grabs a hand fan made out of a torn piece from a cardboard and blows him some air. Momentarily, she looks at the small Mandir hanging on the wall and closes her eyes, bows her head down and thanks god and prays.

For the last 5-7 years, Dabral family was facing financial constraints but it was never this bad but since Samrish was diagnosed with Aplastic Anaemia, all the savings, all the money under their possession was spent after the treatment and cure of Samrish.

CHAPTER TWO

Web of Lies

As Taksh walks in from the elephantine black gate and strolls to the house, he looks around the entire estate in awe, this house was similar to the house of his dreams, as the cool evening breeze dances with the leaves of the well groomed trees on both sides of the walking passage, Taksh remembers the house was somewhat similar to what his family owned for some years when his father's work was at peak before that night of tragic collapse of everything for them. Taksh sees Rao and Isha enjoying their evening tea in the garden, Rao waves at Taksh and asks him to join them, Taksh speeds up his pace of walk; he looks at Isha who was secretly glancing at him too. Isha was a young girl in her late teens with curly hair, brown skin, brown eyes and a small nose, she has uneven teeth but Taksh finds them beautiful and cute.

"Congratulations Dabral sahab, khush raho!" Rao gets up from his seat and hugs Taksh; he offers him a seat. Isha congratulates him too with a fist bump and they both share a warm and wide smile. Isha and Taksh were sweethearts from a long time, Rao was somewhat aware of it too but they never showed any such behaviour before his eyes neither did Rao confront them. As Taksh takes a seat, Rao takes a cup and pours some tea for him but is asked not to, by Isha.

"Dadu baad mein, abhi main iske liye kuch laayi hui ise woh dikhana hai." Isha reveals.

*"toh yahin le aanaa..."*Rao suggests, Isha gives it a thought and tries to come up with another excuse.

"Koi baat nahi sir, main khud jaake le aata hoon," Taksh offers. Rao nods his head, Taksh and Isha saunter inside the house, Samrish wakes up and sees his entire room is pitch black, completely lightless and the power supply is still out, he walks out of the room to the hall and sees candles around the house, he calls out for Pramila. Pramila comes running. *"Bijli abhi tak nahi aayi?"* Samrish inquires.

"woh.. inka kuch khamba wamba gir gaya hai chowk pe sabki bijlee kati hui hai shayad kal ayegi.." Pramila lies. Samrish nods his head and goes to the bathroom, as he urinates into the commode he notices rays of light coming from the small ventilation window of the bathroom. Samrish peeps out and sees all the houses are lit up but his.

He prowls out and looks at Pramila, *"chowk pe khamba gira hai na?"*

Pramila gets a little alert but lies again, Samrish then tries to walk out, *"Ruk main dekh ke aata hoon.."*

"arre aise andhere mein kahan hi jaoge.. rehne do.. waise bhi abhi koi garmi thodi hai sardi ka mausam darwaaze pe hai, raat bhar yunhi kat jayega.." Pramila explains and tries to stop him.

"Kat gayi na Bijli?" Samrish sighs.

Pramila explains how Taksh has said he will take care of it in the morning. Samrish again frowns, *"Bola tha na faltu testo mein paise mat barbaad kar ab woh kahaan se layega.. sarkaari funds aane mein abhi bhi mahine do mahine lagenge."*

Pramila reveals him that Taksh is managing household expenses since months now so it is not a problem. Samrish still doesn't believe anything and helpleslly goes back into the room. "*Khana lagaun?*" Pramila asks.

"*bhookh nahi hai.. tu khaa le.*" Samrish thuds the door.

Isha takes Taksh to her bedroom and gets a wrapped big rectangular box out from her cupboard. Taksh keeps the box on bed and Isha pulls him towards her and arms him around and hugs him. "*This is my gift*", Taksh sighs.

Isha frees herself and asks him to unwrap the gift. Taksh looks at the box and looks at her, then raises his brow, "*Unwrap? Which one?*" Isha hits him on the shoulders and insists him to open the gift.

As Taksh tears apart the wrapping paper, he looks straight into her eyes, she blushes and looks away; the box had a laptop. Taksh gets uncomfortable looking at the price tag, "*I know you can afford it but main ye afford nahi kar sakta Isha, aisi expensive cheezein nahi le paunga main,*" Taksh expresses his discomfort.

"*Afford nahi kar sakta nahi, afford nahi kar sakta tha.. bhoolo mat.. aaj hi subah you have got funding from the government of India.. ab kuch din mein tumhara business shuru ho jayega aur fir tum aise chaar laptop din ke khareedoge..*" Isha relaxes him.

"*woh toh thik hai par din ke chaar laptop khareed ke karunga kya itne laptop ka?*"

Isha hits him again and they both wrap their arms around each other and lean their faces when Rao calls out for Isha and they both hurry out. Isha stops midway and asks Taksh to go, she needs to get him something else.

Taksh smiles at Rao and sits on a chair beside him, Rao looks at the laptop and smiles back. *"Bus kitne baje hai?"* Rao asks.

Taksh utters, *"ab yahan se jaunga 1 ghante baad bus hai, subah tak pounch jaunga."* Taksh and Rao both sip tea.

As Taksh is reminded of home, his mother's call about power cut also strikes his head. He sips down his entire cup and gathers courage and finally shoots his request to Rao as he sees Isha is still inside. *"Sir.."*

"haan bol na.."

"sir.. woh matlab apko toh pata hi hai sarkari process hai.. abhi funds aane mein time lag sakta hai thoda aur.. Bijli kat gayi hai.. paise sare papa ke check up test wagera main lag g—" Taksh hesitantly requests.

"pagal hai kya beta mujhe bataya kar ye sab?" Rao takes his wallet out, *"ye sab me sharmaya mat kar waise bhi kuch din mein tere account mein bhi paise ajayenge.."* Rao counts the money, Taksh looks at him and vaguely smiles.

"kya?Waise...tune sab ready kar liya hai na..company registration aur account khulwale ab...? Ek lawyer dekh woh kardega ye sab..... aur saare kagaz ek jagah dhyaan se rakhna idhar udhar mat karna..." Rao looks up at his face and disappointedly utters, *"Ab kab karega beta?"*

"bas do ek din mein khol lunga.. Papa ke saath jaakar.." Taksh defends. *"Waise kab tak kaam start karenge kuch bataya hai?"* Rao asks again.

"Woh baat toh nahi hui abhi par bola hai kuch dino mein site ki details denge aur cargo India aate hi inform karenge." Taksh tells him.

"Aur documentation?" Rao questions. *"Woh toh Sanath ji dekh lenge unhone bola."*

"Hmmmm.. sambhal ke ye Sanath bhi zyada bharosewala nahi hai," Rao warns him, *"Waise kitne chahiye abhi?"* Rao asks again but by the moment, Isha came out with a packet. As Taksh sees Isha, he signals Rao to keep the money back. After all, borrowing money in front of his lady would hurt his ego/self-respect — whatever you call it!

Isha hands him a packet and says, *"Ghewar hai isme.. aunty ke favourite. Aunty ko hi dena khud mat khaa jaana.. haan agar aunty ke khaane ke baad bache toh khaa lena.."*

"Jo hukum, madam.." Taksh accepts the packet and keeps it on the box of the laptop. All of them chuckle and chitchat for a while meanwhile Rao and Taksh share glances but could not come up with an idea to send Isha away for a couple of minutes.

Rao finally takes an attempt and asks her to bring her medications from inside as he felt uneasy but this too went in vain when Isha replied, *"Khaane se pehle dawai lenge toh fir gas ho jayegi apko chaliye khana khaa lijiye fir le lena dawai.."*

Taksh has barely any time left as he needs to catch the bus to Mohali, with a blue face, he takes leave from them.

Pramila is pouring tea in a cup when the bulb in the kitchen lights up, she immediately closes her eyes, folds her hands and thanks god then gleefully serve tea to her husband; while the couple sip their tea with rusk, Taksh strolls in, Pramila strides to him, takes all the packets keeps them on a side. *"Tukku.. puri Dilli le aya kya beta?"* she asks excitedly.

Taksh touches her feet, hugs her, then greets Samrish, followed by it, Taksh gives his father a new shirt and asks his mother to open the carton, it was a pressure cooker, *"Ye bohot accha kiya.. naya cooker le aya.. puraana wala bas naam ka cooker hai. Pateele ke barar hi kaam karne laga hai."*

Taksh takes money out of his pocket and gives it to Pramila and utters, *"Ration waale ka de dena.."*

"itte paise kahan se laaya tu.. aa gaye kya sarkari funds?" Pramila asks in shock.

"umm.. kuch aisa hi samjho.." Taksh smiles.

Taksh looks at his father and he doesn't seem very happy about it when Taksh asks him the reason, Samrish shoots his question as bullets. Thankfully, Pramila interrupted and asked them to talk about work later, she further commands Taksh to freshen up and take a bath.

Taksh teases his mother about being okay with no bath for weeks and takes the laptop box and walk into the room; he walks back out and informs Pramila, *"Maa... woh Ghewar hai dabbe mein tumhare liye.. aap aur papa khaa lena main khaake aya hoon bus mein hoon.."*

"tere papa ko ab aur Ghewar mat khila... unka sugar waise hi high hai.." Pramila chuckles, Samrish maintains his silence and doesn't say anything.

Taksh is sitting on his bed staring at the laptop box with teared up eyes; he opens the box— it was empty, just the protective thermocol brackets were all that was inside the box. He stares at the empty box as tears roll down his eyes and tear drops fall on the thermocol, he closes the box and slides it under his bed.

Under his bed, was a graveyard of all the empty box of gifts that Isha gave him but he had to sell the laptop that Isha gifted him with her own earnings, but he was helpless as he had to use the money to manage his family expenses. There was a box of cards, letters that

Isha gave him. He didn't sell them, they were one of his priceless possessions.

Taksh sits immobile on the bed for some time, looks upon the noisy ceiling fan moving as fast as an express train at its station; the blades were putting in all the efforts but could barely move; Taksh switches it off, getting rid of the irritating mind-wrenching noise, uncloth himself and walks into the bathroom, adjusts the bucket under the tap, opens the tap and shouts, *"Mummy shampoo hai kya?"*

"Haan sabun ke niche padi hogi." Pramila answers.

Taksh checks under the soap stand and sachets of shampoo were lying there, he checks the temperature of the water by dipping his fingers into the water and shuts the bathroom gate.

As Taksh walks in from the elephantine black gate and strolls to the house, he looks around the entire estate in awe, this house was similar to the house of his dreams, as the cool evening breeze dances with the leaves of the well groomed trees on both sides of the walking passage, Taksh remembers the house was somewhat similar to what his family owned for some years when his father's work was at peak before that night of tragic collapse of everything for them. Taksh sees Rao and Isha enjoying their evening tea in the garden, Rao waves at Taksh and asks him to join them, Taksh speeds up his pace of walk; he looks at Isha who was secretly glancing at him too. Isha was a young girl in her late teens with curly hair, brown skin, brown eyes and a small nose, she has uneven teeth but Taksh finds them beautiful and cute.

"Congratulations Dabral sahab, khush raho!" Rao gets up from his seat and hugs Taksh; he offers him a seat. Isha congratulates him too with a fist bump and they both share a warm and wide smile. Isha and Taksh were sweethearts from a long time, Rao was somewhat aware of it too but they never showed any such behaviour before

his eyes neither did Rao confront them. As Taksh takes a seat, Rao takes a cup and pours some tea for him but is asked not to, by Isha.

"DTukku baad mein, abhi main iske liye kuch laayi hui ise woh dikhana hai." Isha reveals.

"toh yahin le aa naa.." Rao suggests, Isha gives it a thought and tries to come up with another excuse.

"Koi baat nahi sir, main khud jaake le aata hoon," Taksh offers. Rao nods his head, Taksh and Isha saunter inside the house,

Samrish wakes up and sees his entire room is pitch black, completely lightless and the power supply is still out, he walks out of the room to the hall and sees candles around the house, he calls out for Pramila. Pramila comes running. *"Bijli abhi tak nahi aayi?"* Samrish inquires.

"woh.. inka kuch khamba wamba gir gaya hai chowk pe sabki bijlee kati hui hai shayad kal ayegi.." Pramila lies. Samrish nods his head and goes to the bathroom, as he urinates into the commode he notices rays of light coming from the small ventilation window of the bathroom. Samrish peeps out and sees all the houses are lit up but his.

He prowls out and looks at Pramila, *"chowk pe khamba gira hai na?"*

Pramila gets a little alert but lies again, Samrish then tries to walk out, *"Ruk main dekh ke aata hoon.."*

"arre aise andhere mein kahan hi jaoge.. rehne do.. waise bhi abhi koi garmi thodi hai sardi ka mausam darwaaze pe hai, raat bhar yunhi kat jayega.." Pramila explains and tries to stop him.

"Kat gayi na Bijli?" Samrish sighs.

Pramila explains how Taksh has said he will take care of it in the morning. Samrish again frowns, *"Bola tha na faltu testo mein paise mat barbaad kar ab woh kahaan se layega.. sarkaari funds aane mein abhi bhi mahine do mahine lagenge."*

Pramila reveals him that Taksh is managing household expenses since months now so it is not a problem. Samrish still doesn't believe anything and helpeslly goes back into the room. *"Khana lagaun?"* Pramila asks.

"bhookh nahi hai.. tu khaa le." Samrish thuds the door.

Isha takes Taksh to her bedroom and gets a wrapped big rectangular box out from her cupboard. Taksh keeps the box on bed and Isha pulls him towards her and arms him around and hugs him. "This is my gift," Taksh sighs.

Isha frees herself and asks him to unwrap the gift. Taksh looks at the box and looks at her, then raises his brow, *"Unwrap? Which one?"* Isha hits him on the shoulders and insists him to open the gift.

As Taksh tears apart the wrapping paper, he looks straight into her eyes, she blushes and looks away; the box had a laptop. Taksh gets uncomfortable looking at the price tag, *"I know you can afford it but main ye afford nahi kar sakta Isha, aisi expensive cheezein nahi le paunga main,"* Taksh expresses his discomfort.

"Afford nahi kar sakta nahi, afford nahi kar sakta tha.. bhoolo mat.. aaj hi subah you have got funding from the government of India.. ab kuch din mein tumhara business shuru ho jayega aur fir tum aise chaar laptop din ke khareedoge.." Isha relaxes him.

"woh toh thik hai par din ke chaar laptop khareed ke karunga kya itne laptop ka?"

Isha hits him again and they both wrap their arms around each other and lean their faces when Rao calls out for Isha and they both hurry out. Isha stops midway and asks Taksh to go, she needs to get him something else.

Taksh smiles at Rao and sits on a chair beside him, Rao looks at the laptop and smiles back. *"Bus kitne baje hai?"* Rao asks.

Taksh utters, *"ab yahan se jaunga 1 ghante baad bus hai, subah tak pounch jaunga."* Taksh and Rao both sip tea.

As Taksh is reminded of home, his mother's call about power cut also strikes his head. He sips down his entire cup and gathers courage and finally shoots his request to Rao as he sees Isha is still inside. *"Sir.."*

"haan bol na.."

"sir.. woh matlab apko toh pata hi hai sarkari process hai.. abhi funds aane mein time lag sakta hai thoda aur.. Bijli kat gayi hai.. paise sare papa ke check up test wagera main lag g—" Taksh hesitantly requests.

"pagal hai kya beta mujhe bataya kar ye sab?" Rao takes his wallet out, *"ye sab me sharmaya mat kar waise bhi kuch din mein tere account mein bhi paise ajayenge.."* Rao counts the money, Taksh looks at him and vaguely smiles.

"kya? Waise... tune sab ready kar liya hai na.. company registration aur account khulwale ab...? Ek lawyer dekh woh kardega ye sab..... aur saare kagaz ek jagah dhyaan se rakhna idhar udhar mat karna..." Rao looks up at his face and disappointedly utters, *"Ab kab karega beta?"*

"bas do ek din mein khol lunga.. Papa ke saath jaakar.." Taksh defends.

"Waise kab tak kaam start karenge kuch bataya hai?" Rao asks again.

"Woh baat toh nahi hui abhi par bola hai kuch dino mein site ki details denge aur cargo India aate hi inform karenge." Taksh tells him.

"Aur documentation?" Rao questions.

"Woh toh Sanath ji dekh lenge unhone bola."

"Hmmmm.. sambhal ke ye Sanath bhi zyada bharosewala nahi hai," Rao warns him, *"Waise kitne chahiye abhi? "* Rao asks again but by the moment, Isha came out with a packet. As Taksh sees Isha, he signals Rao to keep the money back. After all, borrowing money in front of his lady would hurt his ego/self-respect — whatever you call it!

Isha hands him a packet and says, *"Ghewar hai isme.. aunty ke favourite. Aunty ko hi dena khud mat khaa jaana.. haan agar aunty ke khaane ke baad bache toh khaa lena.."*

"Jo hukum, madam.." Taksh accepts the packet and keeps it on the box of the laptop. All of them chuckle and chitchat for a while meanwhile Rao and Taksh share glances but could not come up with an idea to send Isha away for a couple of minutes.

Rao finally takes an attempt and asks her to bring her medications from inside as he felt uneasy but this too went in vain when Isha replied, *"Khaane se pehle dawai lenge toh fir gas ho jayegi apko chaliye khana khaa lijiye fir le lena dawai.."*

Taksh has barely any time left as he needs to catch the bus to Mohali, with a blue face, he takes leave from them.

Pramila is pouring tea in a cup when the bulb in the kitchen lights up, she immediately closes her eyes, folds her hands and thanks god then gleefully serve tea to her husband; while the couple sip their tea with rusk, Taksh strolls in, Pramila strides to him, takes all the packets keeps them on a side. "*Tukku.. puri Dilli le aya kya beta?*" she asks excitedly.

Taksh touches her feet, hugs her, then greets Samrish, followed by it, Taksh gives his father a new shirt and asks his mother to open the carton, it was a pressure cooker, "*Ye bohot accha kiya.. naya cooker le aya.. puraana wala bas naam ka cooker hai. Pateele ke barar hi kaam karne laga hai.*"

Taksh takes money out of his pocket and gives it to Pramila and utters, "*Ration waale ka de dena..*"

"*itte paise kahan se laaya tu.. aa gaye kya sarkari funds?*" Pramila asks in shock.

"*umm.. kuch aisa hi samjho..*" Taksh smiles.

Taksh looks at his father and he doesn't seem very happy about it when Taksh asks him the reason, Samrish shoots his question as bullets. Thankfully, Pramila interrupted and asked them to talk about work later, she further commands Taksh to freshen up and take a bath.

Taksh teases his mother about being okay with no bath for weeks and takes the laptop box and walk into the room; he walks back out and informs Pramila, "*Maa... woh Ghewar hai dabbe mein tumhare liye.. aap aur papa khaa lena main khaake aya hoon bus mein hoon..*"

"*tere papa ko ab aur Ghewar mat khila... unka sugar waise hi high hai..*" Pramila chuckles, Samrish maintains his silence and doesn't say anything.

Taksh is sitting on his bed staring at the laptop box with teared up eyes; he opens the box— it was empty, just the protective thermocol brackets were all that was inside the box. He stares at the empty box as tears roll down his eyes and tear drops fall on the thermocol, he closes the box and slides it under his bed.

Under his bed, was a graveyard of all the empty box of gifts that Isha gave him but he had to sell the laptop that Isha gifted him with her own earnings, but he was helpless as he had to use the money to manage his family expenses. There was a box of cards, letters that Isha gave him. He didn't sell them, they were one of his priceless possessions.

Taksh sits immobile on the bed for some time, looks upon the noisy ceiling fan moving as fast as an express train at its station; the blades were putting in all the efforts but could barely move; Taksh switches it off, getting rid of the irritating mind-wrenching noise, uncloth himself and walks into the bathroom, adjusts the bucket under the tap, opens the tap and shouts, "*Mummy shampoo hai kya?*"

"*Haan sabun ke niche padi hogi.*" Pramila answers.

Taksh checks under the soap stand and sachets of shampoo were lying there, he checks the temperature of the water by dipping his fingers into the water and shuts the bathroom gate.

CHAPTER THREE

Dilemma and Desires

The entire Dabral family is sitting on the dining table; Pramila serves food to everyone and takes a plate for herself too; Taksh takes a bite and feels the taste to the core. Pramila thinks her son missed home food and is now enjoying it but Taksh could barely manage his expenses in Delhi and would often skip eating and was settled for just one meal a day except for the days his friends or Imran would pay for lunch or if he visited their homes. Taksh's parents had no idea that their son was starving in Delhi and was also hospitalised once due to lack of proper food but like half of his life, Taksh kept all of it hidden. Things were really not this way until Samrish fell to bed, before that they were well off to food and shelter but with passing time, Samrish's health and their financial strains were only worsening.

Pramila and Samrish inquire about Taksh about all the details, Samrish is still unsure if his son was telling the truth. Pramila is the happiest of the three as her son has come back after months and their longing dream was finally about to come true.

Since Taksh was to receive so much money, both his parents have become ivestment consultants and are advising Taksh to invest the money in a safe place. Samrish like every fathe asks him to opt for a fixed deposit but his mother, Pramila wants his son to deposit the money in a post office. Back in the day, post office saving schemes were very popular and were operational at all metro cities to rural villages. Followed by it, Taksh and Samrish make jokes on Pramila for her advice that doesn't count as she keeps her money in food containers in the kitchen.

As he takes another bite, he keeps his elbows on the table and table jerks a little, Pramila smiles, *"ye table bhi badalni padegi..kitna bhi kagaz thoos lo iske pairo ke neeche humesha upar neeche hi rehti hai.."*

"Le lenge, maa." Taksh sighs.

Samrish ahems, *"Just because you have startes earning, you do not have to spend it all"*, sips some water and continues, *"Save some, At least, 30% of your salary. Waise kitna de rahe hai abhi?"*

Pramila and Taksh stare at Samrish eating and waiting for his answer, he looks at his wife and son staring at him, *"Chutkula yaad aya hai toh mujhe bhi bolo,* I'll also laugh a little."

"Nahi. Aise hi," Taksh takes some more rice and sagg into his plate.

Pramila and Taksh look at each other and smile again, they were happy for Samrish was speaking in english and he would often do it only when he is happy or in a good mood and this time he was doing it after so long that they can't recall the last time he was talking like that. By this time Samrish asks his son again, "Never ask a man his weigh: I know it too.. *par baap ko bol sakte hai..*"

"Woh papa, abhi fixed nahi hai waise thik thaak de dete hai 10 ke aas paas.. ek micro technology company hai.. IBM jaisi.." Taksh lies.

"Dekh.. mujhe jitna zindagi ne sikhaya.. tujhe bhi utna hi sikha sakta hoon.. main apne baap se nahi sikha par tu apne baap se sikh aur naukri mat chodhna jab tak company operations na start kar le. " Samrish advices.

"Oho, rehne bhi do... ye sab choodho naa.. tu bata wahan kya hua, tu mila pradhan mantri ji se, bohot kam bolte hai nahi? Tere se baat ki?" Pramila cuts Samrish down and throws her questions instead.

"Nahi unse toh nahi mila—" Taksh mistakenly speaks the truth then manages the situation, *"Lekin American Rashtrapati aya tha toh usise haal chaal puch aya... kya maaa tum bhi."* This was the only thing Taksh hated to do to anybody and the most to his parents: Lie. He would never lie to his parents but only if he had that choice to make, most of the times, Taksh was helpless, his chest would contract into singularity from within but he had to and exactly that is what he did this time as well.

"Still share with us what exactly happened?" Samrish asked again. This time Taksh explained things in detail about his presentation, performed a demo of the prototype and explained how they would compact it even more and make it function even faster. He then garnished his story with a sprinkle of lies and went on saying things like the PM and a few other officers were all so impressed they all clapped and immediately liked the presentation, the Pm then asked about Samrish and even offered an apology for whatsoever happened in 98 and he also added that PM advised him to take advice of his father in the business. Samrish's eyes lit up with joy as he hears this from his son. Samrish even reconfirmed if it really happened and Taksh lied again on his face.

There were violent knocks on the door, it was the kiranawala. Samrish attempts to get up but Taksh stops him and hints at his mother. Pramila immediately took the cash out from one of the dabbas of daal in the kitchen and opens the door; before he could humiliate them any further she offered him the entire due. The temperament of the kiranawala completely changed and with a wide fake smile, he asked, *"Kuch aur chahiye kya parjai? Bhijwau ladke se?"* Pramila shook her head with a smile and shut the door on his face and joined Taksh and Samrish on the dining table.

Samrish again advises Taksh to invest and spend the money wisely as at his age it is very easy to get trapped in impulse buying.

"ufff.. yaar kya yaar aap bhi.. 10 hazar honge mushkil se isme Zirakpur mein kothi baandh du kya?" Taksh gets up and goes to the basin to wash his hands.

"tab fir meri baat maano dall ke dabbe mein hi rehne do." Pramila takes the last bite, sips her glass empty and takes all the plates together and goes to the kitchen sink, arranges the plates and bowls there and washes her hands in the same sink.

Samrish and Taksh are walking alongside through the flea market, Samrish is carrying two full bags of vegetables. Every other person in the market is greeting Samrish and asks about his whereabouts as he is seen less often. Samrish is repeating the same answer to everyone — *"woh tabiyat nazuk chal rahi si.. hun'd.. baaki sab changa si.."*

Samrish reconfirms again, *"sun.. sahi mein woh maan gaye ya teri maa ke aage awein bol raha tha?"*

"Nahi papa sahi mein, haan.. mushkil tha lekin hogaya.. unhone khud bharosa dilaya iss bar India ka apna semiconductor plant hoga alag se kuch 30 hazar crore ka budget banaya hai government ne." Taksh explains.

"Dekh.. fir bhi sambhal ke apne upar kuch zimmedari mat lena jab tak funding naa ajaye inka koi bharosa nahi pehle bhi bohot baar—"

"ab pehle jaisa kuch nahi hai.. ye sarkar bohot aage ka sochke steps leti hai aur PM sahab khud finance mein the woh ye sab acche se samajhte hai ki aaj agar India ko world power banana hai toh India ki apni silicon

valley banani padegi.. Saare initial setup ke machinery bhi USA se order kar di hai. Cargo India aate hi kaam shuru hoga, abhi humare Punjab ke CM sahab se bhi milne jaana hai woh site allot karenge." On hearing all the details Samrish breathes in peace but still advises Taksh to keep a check on everything at regular intervals because Samrish knew it better that Mr. Singh was just the face of the PM, the real power belonged to somebody else in the ruling party. Taksh then asks his father if he may need the patent files as it is required to achieve such chips before others. But Samrish just bluntly denies it and asks him to figure it out himself as he doesn't want to get involved in this. A disappointed Taksh doesn't say much.

"Aap bag do main pakadta hoon." Taksh tries to get the bags from his father.

"Abhi itna kamzor nahi hua hoon.. ki tujhe baap banna pade.." Samrish stops him.

As the father and son take a turn into the narrow lanes, they see an infant crying while his mother is trying to get him down from his father's scooter. *"Utar puttar.. mainu late ho jaana hai fer.."* His father was also trying to console him but the kid was crying like there was no tomorrow and he was seeing his father for the last time.

The bawling of the kid was so loud and shriek, the soundwave transformed into a time machine and took Samrish back into his childhood.

1962:

Lokbhushan was packing his clothes in a metal trunk, on the side he was also dressing up. Samrish was sketching something in his drawing book but when he realized his father was leaving somewhere, he began squalling at his highest, Rakshit had him on his lap and was trying all known tactics to stop him from crying.

Lokbhushan was a single parent, his wife died a couple of years ago during the Influenza outbreak in India. He lost his parents in pre- independence India in one of the last clashes with the Britishers before they left India. Lokbhushan and Samrish only had each other, Rakshit was their only family, relative, friend, whatever you call him. Lokbhushan was devastated and dispirited after the government chose not to stand with their words. Lokbhushan took up Fairkid's offer for a job in their new Malaysia manufacturing plant. The odd part was: Lokbhushan and Rakshit both had the offer; both of them followed up on it but only Lokbhushan was selected and he did not share any detail with his friend instead asked him for a promise to take care of Samrish for a few years until he returns. He sweared on Samrish that he would come back soon and then start their own factory with their own money.

"*Par veere tera appointment letter kittho hai?*" Rakshit inquires.

"*woh fairkid walo ka koi banda leke airport hi aayega... baaki sara paperwork wahin karenge Malaysia mein.*" Lokbhushan explained.

"*khyaal rakhi veere... jo bhi ho hai taa akhir gore hi.. mera piyo kehnda si inn goro naal bharosa apna pair khud khulaadi pe de maarne barabar hai.. upar se desh bhi naya..*" Rakshit warns him of the odds.

"*desh naya nahi hai.. bas naam naya hai..*" Lokbhushan takes some money out from the locker.

"*Malay-sia. Soch gar bharat da naam bhi aise kar de? Bharat-sia..*" Rakshit chuckled.

"*bharat nahi.. India-sia..*" they both cracked up. Samrish is constantly crying, Lokbhushan takes him on his lap as he sits beside Rakshit. He starts consoing Samrish; a bus ticket dropped from his pocket it was from Delhi to Wagah border. Rakshit questions him but Lokbhushan gets a little uncomfortable and excuses himself by telling him that he had to meet someone and then they both were to leave together for Malaysia.

But Rakshit confronts him again, *"par tu toh bol raha tha plane aaj dophar ki hai."*

"arre aaj dophar nikalna hai bola tha plane toh kal ki hai." Lokbhushan uttered.

"laa teri ticket dikhaa zara." Rakshit raised his brow.

"abe wohi toh lene jaa raha hoon uss bande pe hai sab woh ayega fir hum ticket katenge aur niklenge.. tu ye chor ye paise rakh main mahine mahine baaki bhejta rahunga." Lokbhushan changed the topic.

"veere.. kya bol raha hai? thoda apne aap ko sun.. kya bande pe ticket hai fir tum dono aake ticket kaatoge.." Rakshit doubted.

"arre bhai us bande pe plane ki ticket hai ab main jaunga fir wapas dilli aane ki ticket hum dono kaatenge fir niklenge.. yaaar zyada bamkesh na ban.. der ho rahi hai nikalne de." Lokbhushan once again kisses Samrish's forehead and tells him he will be back soon and not to trouble Rakshit much, eat his food, go to school and write letters to him. He carefully puts Samrish on the bed as he still cries and grabs him to not let go. Lokbhushan released himself from the grip of Samrish's hands, hugs Rakshit and tells him to take care of himself and Samrish, followed by which, he walks out with the trunk.

Samrish began bawling like crazy, Rakshit was suspicious too. He made Samrish sit on the bed again and went on to check the drawers of Lokbhushan's study table. To his fear, he found the passport of Lokbhushan inside the drawer which made it evident that Lokbhushan went wherever but Malaysia. He looked at the passport and then the whimpering face of Samrish.

Later, he tried searching for him everywhere, even in some places of Pakistan as he doubted Lokbhushan went to Pakistan to present the semiconductor idea to the Pakistani government but no trace of Lokbhushan was found. That was the last day Samrish saw his father.

Later, Rakshit raised Samrish as his own son, he chose not to marry as another family would distract him from upbringing Samrish. Rakshit became his father and his parents loved Samrish as their grandson till they were alive. As Samrish grew up, Rakshit also became a mentor and business partner when they both set up STL, together.

CHAPTER FOUR

Commencement of Chaos

Pramila puts the key in the lock, unlocks the door. Samrish barges inside the house and growls, *"mazaak bana ke rakha hai behanch... koi matlab hota hai iska batao.."*

Taksh was paying the taxi driver, he offeed him a 100 rupee note but the driver insisted on more. Taksh offered another 50 but the driver was asking for more. *"paa ji itne ka toh petrol bhi nahi laga hoga.. upar se gaadi bhi sarkaari hai..CM sahab ki."*

"tabhi toh paise bhi zyada maang raha hoon.. CM sahab ki gaadi hai thoda badhake do.. ab roz roz thodi baithoge isme.." The driver taunts. Growls and screams of Samrish was audible till the road, Taksh puts another 50 into the driver's pocket and hops down from the car.

He marches inside and sees a furious Samrish walking back and forth in the hall room. Samrish frowns at Taksh, *"tere ko bhi bola tha na matt pad in sab mein. ye saale dogle hote hai.. bas apna dekhte hai."*

"Papa! Thik hai koi baat nahi.. aisa bhi kya gussaṢ Itni badi baat thodi haiṢ" Taksh tried to calm him down but he comes at him and is about to slap Taksh but Pramila walks between and stops him, she asks Taksh to go inside his room as he walks in and closes the door slowly, Samrish grabs the spatula kept on the dining table and hits Pramila with it.

"sau baar tereko bhi bola tha.. mat badhawa de ise lekin tune bhi mere se saari baat chupaayi.. iska bhi dekhiyo wohi haal hoga jo mere baap ka hua, mera hua ab iska hone wala hai.. "

It was the day of Taksh's board results and he scored happy numbers. Pramila was very happy so was Samrish but his grief overpowered his happiness as he had lost all that he created just a year back and they had shifted to this small colony house and are struggling to meet ends. Although, Samrish wanted a grand celebration for his son on his board results but situations weren't letting him to do so and a man who has lost everything one after the other is supposed to be a hopeless man and exactly that was what Samrish was down to — a hopeless griefing man who missed out on the small happinesses of life too as his sorrow had him engulfed wholly.

And that day, grief decided to stab him once again when Taksh revealed he wished to take Science stream for his higher secondary and plans to pursue electronic engineering. When Samrish asked him the specific reason, he clearly mentioned he wanted to set up another semiconductor factory as he has studied the past failures and wants to solve the problem his way and return back everything that his father lost. Samrish on the other side wanted Taksh to stay away from the semiconductor bullshit that ruined his father and him. He suggested rather commanded Taksh to take up commerce and opt for Chartered Accountancy, it was a promising secured career. Taksh was adamant on taking up science even Pramila convinced Samrish to let him do what he wants it must be god's plan. Samrish still did not want him to get his hands dirty into the sewage of Semiconductor and everything. He allowed Taksh to take science only on the condition to take science and pursue engineering if he would choose any other stream of engineering except electronics. Taksh promised him the same but later went to Delhi for his education and chose exactly that he promised he would not.

Samrish was not informed, Pramila was aware of it but she hid it too and when finally Samrish was told about it, it was too late.

During his college, He was accompanied by another obsessive failure, Imran who wanted to do something for semiconductor production in India and idealised Taksh's father for he was the first person to run a semiconductor corporation, in fact, a successful one albeit for a short span. Imran helped Taksh with a lot of things and he was the one who told Taksh about a lot of things that his father did for the nation and was never credited for. Those stories sparked the obsession inside Taksh to get his father everything he lost.

Imran was into college politics, he contacted politicians and party worker at every level and introduced Sanath to Taksh who formed a bridge between the PMO and Taksh. Imran was also unaware of the exact post or Sanath but he was very close ally of a member of parliament, more of an event organiser for the politician and the politician was further connected to the PM's cabinet of ministers and this was how the entire chain was formed and the presentation/ project report reached the desk of the PM himself.

And then trusting a fresh graduate with such a cardinal matter was very unlikely. That was when a mysterious stranger took the guarantee upon him and only after the stranger's intervention, PMO took Taksh seriously. Taksh was unaware of the identity of the stranger but just knew he was a friend of his father and trusted Taksh's capabilities only because of Samrish's blood in Taksh's veins.

Samrish was still shouting, *"Koi matlab hota hai... bar bar bulaake aise bina mile bhej dena.. hum itne faltu hai kya? Hume koi kaam nahi hai? Cm hai toh kya ye karenge? Ek Cm the humare time pe Zail Singh*

ji aur ek yee hai..par dusro kya bolna jab apna hi beta dhoka de toh?"
Samrish smirks.

Samrish was angry and was broiling in rage because this was the third time in 2 months. He had to come back from the CM house without being able to meet him, whereas he was made to wait for hours along with his wife and son. Taksh was also clueless as to why this treatment was given to them.

It was stressing him more as almost 8 had passed since the meeting and neither had the cargo delivery happened nor had any funds transferred into his bank account from any government source. Moreover, meanwhile the delivery takes its time and course, he was to be allotted a site for the factory and with the initial funds, the setup was to be started but surprisingly nothing of what was said was done. Moreover, Taksh had been lying to his parents and everyone else that the government is sending some money but all is getting invested in the factory setup, he was managing his expenses by borrowing money from everyone and told them that the money was to come soon, the cargo is stuck at the port for some customs issues and as this was backed by national media houses too, everyone believed him. Samrish was the one who was getting as anxious as Taksh if not more, about the entire thing. Every now and then, he would ask Taksh about updates, force him to complete paperwork, and force him to show him the land that was allotted. Taksh would deny it every time and make an excuse which was raising suspicion for Samrish even more.

The CM of Punjab was to invite Taksh to his residence for the land allotment and paperwork regarding the initial set up. And when Samrish found out about it he forced Taksh to take him and Pramila along.. and then Taksh tried to get an appointment a number of times but would fail so eventually he decided and would take his parents along without an appointment. And as per his plan they were asked to wait and were eventually sent home.

But this time, the CM saw them but told Taksh, he is yet to receive any update from the centre and is waiting for it. He assures Taksh that sometimes, these things take time and Taksh should be patient after all it was a matter of huge financing. A lot of things were to be taken care of. He even greeted his parents and send his driver to drop them home but Samrish was angry because now he knew that Taksh was lying about the paperwork and the land allotment as the cargo that was to be delivered for the factory setup for semiconductor chip manufacturing was stuck at the ports for some customs' complications. He was furious at Taksh and was equally mad at the government as he sensed the same history repeating again. Even Imran and Taksh's team that helped him develop the prototype were all giving up hopes and Taksh was trying all that he could to keep them hopeful but in reality, he was losing faith too.

In the past few months, after the initial delays, he tried to contact Sanath and even get an appointment at the PM office but nothing worked. He even took a few trips to Delhi but no update was available nor was anyone available whom he could talk to about the matter. And after today's incident, it was barely possible to be patient any longer.

Taksh wakes up and takes a tour around the house to estimate the mood of his father; Pramila was equally upset but still believed there must have been a reason for his son choosing to lie about things. Samrish was not talking to anyone. Taksh slowly begins to walk back in when there's a knock at the door. Taksh's mother opens the door, Taksh is staggered to see Harman. He asks him to come inside but Harman asks Taksh to come out for a minute, there was something important. Pramila offers both of them to go inside Taksh's room and talk in private but Harman insists Taksh come out. Taksh did, as they both walk a few hundred foot away, Taksh is bombshelled; flabbergasted to see Isha. He saunters and stands right before her, he looks around, there was nobody, he hugs Isha;

Isha doesn't hug him back.

"Tum yahan, main toh soch bhi nahi sakta—" Taksh expresses joy. *"Main bhi soch hi nahi sakti.."* Isha cuts him amid his words. *"Tum dono ek dusre ko kaise jaante ho?"* Taksh queries Isha.

"Bhai tune jo woh laptop becha tha na Fayaz bhai ko.. woh asal mein unke kisi bande ne Isha ke hi cousin ko bech diya.." Harman reveals.

"accha woh.. jo mujhse gum gaya tha? becha kya tha bhai?" Taksh tries to handle the situation.

"mat kar.. fayda nahi hai.. maine ki thi koshish.." Harman stops him from lying further.

"uss laptop ko maine apne savings se khareeda tha...aur woh India mein bohot rare hai jaldi milta bhi nahi.. aur tumne 1 din mein... beche diya? Kam se kam gift soch ke rakh lete..." Isha was grinning in anger.

Taksh did not say anything further. Isha began to doubt if it was not the first gift he sold. Taksh then tells them the entire truth, Isha then glares at him. *"tum mujhse maang lete, isse maang lete.. arre dadu se maang lete.. main maang ke de deti. Tumhe kya lagta hai mujhe nahi pata dadu tumhe paise dete hai? Taksh itne diye thode aur dedete par gifts toh nahi bechte na.."* Isha weeps, returns him the letters that he wrote to her and a diary that he gifted her, she snivels and runs away towards the main road.

"Sorry bhai.. I tried." Harman runs behind Isha. Taksh was slowly been devoured by bad luck, he froze there for sometime but the most soul horrendous one was waiting for him, back home.

Taksh comes back home and walks straight into his room, unending calls to Isha; texts to call back: Taksh was craving to connect to her when Samrish calls him out, he ignores him but when his mother bangs his door, he screams, *"Papa abhi nahi ruko.. emergency hai"*

"Bahar aaa.." Samrish commands him; as Taksh walks out, Samrish throws the newspaper at his face. *"Sach boliyo.. tujhe ye bhi pata tha naa.."*

Taksh picks up the newspaper and sees the article that read — **"CARGO CARRYING MACHINERY FOR SEMICONDUCTOR CHIP MANUFACTURING STUCK IN INDIAN PORT FOR 1 YEAR IS REDIRECTED TOWARDS CHINA. CHINA WELCOMES THE SEMICONDUCTOR GIANTS TO INVEST IN CHINA WITH OPEN ARMS AND OFFERS THEM A SECURED PASSAGE FOR TRADE AND OPERATIONS..."**

CHAPTER FIVE

Ghosted by Government

Taksh sat on the bench beside a tea stall; to his right was the road towards Prime Minister's Office, and he was staring just at his right into oblivion. Harman passes him a glass of tea and sits beside him. "*Fir kuch pata chala?*" Harman asks as he warms his warms his palms by holding the hot glass in his grip.

"*2 din se bas ghum hi raha hoon... Imran bhai gaye hai dekhte hai kuch juggad bithaane... Pata nahi kis wajah se sab kaam end moment par atak jata hai, dusri taraf papa bhi apni zidd par ade hue hai, bilkul bharosa nahi raha unhe iss government par.*"Taksh mutters as he knows his father has lost hopes and blames government for the family's financial hardship.

Taksh and Harman's phones rang breaking the silence. It was Pramila's call on Taksh's phone, Harman keeps his phone down and utters after a long breath, "*Yaar main milta hoon tujhse shaam ko abhi university ke liye nikalna padega thoda.. thoda kaam hai.*"

Taksh sits there waiting for Imran and empties three more cups of tea, Pramila was calling on his phone again, Taksh rejects the call again as he could sense it was his father who was on the other side of the phone and if he picks it up, Samrish would add more to his trouble by asking about updates and that is what Taksh did not have, at least at that very moment. Ignorance was his only open door.

It has been two days since Taksh was taken around at different government bodies and ministries that were responsible and associated with his project.. he was denied any meeting with anyone at any level, and he couldn't go back home without an update, his parents were now dependent upon him, and he didn't really have any update nor a fixed job. Due to a lack of updates, Taksh was ignoring calls from his home as well. Taksh was walking around the inside of the gurdwara wondering, about and planning his next move.

Taksh receives a call; Taksh assumes it to be from his home, so he ignores it and continues to ignore it until he sees the caller name, which is Rao. As Taksh picks up, Rao asks him if he had managed to get any update from anybody. Taksh, with a lowered face, *"Kahan se update milega? Koi milne ko tayyar hi nahi hai, samajh hi nahi aa raha kya karun"*

"Tu kahan hai abhi?" Rao asks.

"IESA office ke paas.." Taksh says.

"Thik hai tu jaldi ghar aaja.. main kuch karne ki koshish karta hoon." Rao demands. Taksh confirmed that he will be there in 30-40 minutes and ended the call.

Rao is scolding him when Isha walks in. She glances at Taksh and turns her face away when Taksh glances back. She walks into her bedroom and closes her door. Rao stops for a moment and drinks some water. Taksh apologises.

"Ekdum hi paraya kar diya Dabral sahab.. itna uncle uncle kehte ho aur fir bhi...ye suluk kiya.. mere ghar pehle ana chahiye tha na?" Rao sounds upset, he leans back on his chair and cleans his glasses. Taksh apologises again and keeps his head down.

Rao then offers him lunch and tells him to relax as he had some friends in the government, thanks to Rao's father, who was well connected with the congress leaders post-independence and even during the pre-independence era and he has requested an appointment for him and has been able to get confirmation. Sanath will come and pick him up from Rao's house tomorrow. Rao strictly commands him to sleepover at his place and not leave the main gate until Sanath comes.

After his lunch, he strolls around the hall outside Isha's room, hoping for her to come out and talk once, but she does not open her door for once until dinner. Rao calls out for her and Taksh. She opens the gate and walks straight to the dining table, she ignores Taksh completely. Taksh fails to initiate a conversation during dinner. Rao, when he sees both of them not talking, he senses something wrong but does not interfere. After dinner, Isha helps Rao with medicines. Greets Rao, goodnight and, walks back into her room and locks it from inside. Rao asks Taksh about it, but Taksh shakes his head and smiles a bit, faking having no knowledge about it.

Rao greets him goodnight and leaves, Taksh calls Isha, but she cuts his call and switches her mobile off. Taksh takes a walk.

Soon after, the next day, Rao manages Sanath to meet Taksh...

"You should have at least answered the phone, sir.. maine. Maine kam se kam 100 baar phone kiya hoga." Taksh charges at Sanath. Sanath breathes heavily as they both sit inside his car, and the car is stops in the service lane. *"Itni saari baaton ke baad, the government just backed off.. main wahan umeed mein baitha hoon ki ab hoga tab hoga.. gharwaalo se leke apni team tak sabko jhoothi umeed pe khada rakha hua tha.. aur mujhe hi khabar nahi hai ki.. sarkar ne fir apna faisla badal diya."* Taksh's dissatisfaction was clear as water in his voice.

"*Sarkar majboor hai, bohot soch samajh ke ek ek cheez karni padti hai.*" Sanath explains.

"*Exactly, kis baat ko lekar itni majboori hai ?* What is stopping them to take a step which will make our country powerful and grow economically too. They have the power they can change destiny of crores with just a stroke of a pen but yes only if they intent to, they have to be worthy and accountable to common people and our country as the money spent for their salaries and their VVIP well being comes from the pocket of every honest citizen."

"*Ab factory ki site allot hogi ye sochke mahino chakkar katne ke baad CM batate hai ki unhe centre se confirmation hi nahi hai.. itna halla gulla ho jaane ke baad saal bhar se cargo port pe atka hua hai aur ab China chala gaya waah..*"

"*He is not totally wrong.. pata nahi kyu yeh govermnet bass puri duniya se karza lene mei kyu focused hai..*" Sanath mutters he immediately realises Taksh is right next to him and tries changing topic, " *It is not that simple har front par foreign pressure hai, filhaal isme main tumhari koi help nahi kar sakta,* I suggest you also stop wasting time, *mere contact se permanent government job lagvata hoon tumhari..*

"*Wow.. main yaha pura ecosystem set karne ke plans ke saath ready hoon* which can create thousands of job oppurtunities *aur aap ulta mujhe hi job offer kar rahe hai.* You are not getting my point at all, once these chips manufacturing starts in India it will be a game changer for every sector. *Yeh baat mujh jaise ko samajh aa rahi hai toh power and position par baithe hue so called leaders ko kyu nahi*" Taksh expresses his annoyance, his phone rings he sees Pramila's number and disconnects.

Sanath is in deep thoughts listening to Taksh's visionary statement, he notices the resemblance of father and son as he closely worked with Samrish too but he is helpless as he knew that the governing family is not at all interested in development of the semi-con industry. For escaping the oddness Sanath notices the time in his wrist watch as says " *mujhe ek meeting ke liye der ho rahi hai.. tumhe rao sahab ke wahan drop kardu ?*"

Taksh opens the door in anger and hops out from the car, his phone rings again, he disconnects again. The car dispels away. Pramila is calling Taksh again. Taksh squinches his face and answers it this time, he puts the phone to his ears and utters, "*Haan papa..*"

But nobody speaks from the other side, after hello-ing for quite a few times, Taksh could hear his mother ululating on the other side of the phone, Taksh questions again.

"*Tukku.. jaldi ghar aa.. yeh kuch bol nahi rahe.. uth nahi rahe.. jaldi.. beta.. suniye Tukku aa raha hai uthye.. beta tere papa...*" Pramila weeps, then sobs, then howls on the phone.

CHAPTER SIX

Farewell to the Father

The pyre was fired up and blazing; lifeless body of Samrish was ensnared in the flames that was slowly devouring his flesh and bones along with the woods of the pyre. Taksh, Imran, Harman, Rao along with few others were standing around Samrish. Since the time, Taksh performed mukhagni and fire gorbed his father, he was trying hard to not look at him but the thought that he will not see him ever again was wrenching his heart, something was scratching him from inside, wounding not just his body, but his soul. A clamorous and ear-splitting scream was all he desired at that very moment but his pharynx was numb. He wanted to but couldn't speak or scream or cry. All of them stood in silence beside Taksh. At one corner stood the pandit chanting mantras and just behind the pyre were two chaps who are always present in such cremation grounds and assist you with the arrangements and other chores during the last rites. They stood their with a bamboo rod, giggling, gossiping. They were occasionally hitting on the skull of the burning body, the hits were so hard that it broke the skull into pieces. Taksh got very uncomfortable atthe sight. He was just about to intervene when Rao grabbed him and relaxed him. Taksh looked at Rao with red, swollen, watery eyes and then looked back at his father. No sooner did he look back, a more uncomfortable sight awaited him — the burning body sat up on the pyre, it was just bones and some flesh now. Taksh called out and strode to the pyre, "*Papa...*" everybody held him and pulled him back. the two men hit the sitting skeleton and the ribs broke down and it collapsed back to its initial position.

Neighbour ladies were whispering among themselves, Isha was right beside Pramila who was looking at everyone with restless eyes. Her face had dried up tear marks on the cheeks but her eyes were dry as anything. She gets up from the floor and walks into the kitchen, Isha follows her. Pramila starts making tea for everyone, Isha offers to do it while other ladies offer a hand too but Pramila did not let anyone do it for her.

Taksh, Harman, Imran and Rao get down from Rao's car and walk inside. Taksh offers everyone to sit and paved a carpet for all of them. Pramila comes with tea for everyone and offers it to all as Rao takes the cup, he asks Pramila if she was alright, Pramila looked up at his face and smiles. She kept looking at him for some seconds then continued. Isha asked Taksh about him and gripped his hand tightly... Harman and Imran also asked to leave. *"tum log mere saath chal lena.. "* Rao offered.

"nahi sir.. aap hume emergency mein aate time apne saath le aaye kaafi hai.. aur pareshaan nahi karenge hum apko.." Imran uttered.

"pareshaan kay? Main bhi Dilli hi jaunga, gaadi mein waise bhi 4 log aye the.. chaaro chale bhi jayenge waise hi.. kyun alag jana hai?" Rao questioned, both gave in. Then Rao kept the tea aside and walked to Taksh and told him, *"Sun.. kuch bhi lage bina kisi sankoch ke maang liyo.. tu mere pote se kamm nahi hai.. samjha.. aur ye rakh filhal.."* All of them walk out.

"Main pounch ke phone karti hoon.." Isha said as he walked out.. All of them asked him to take care of Pramila and his own self. The car revved and drove off.

A few weeks later, few college friends of Taksh arrived. Taksh offered them to sit and then apologised to them. *"Sorry yaar.. maine apne saath tumhara bhi pura saal kharab kar diya.. tum sab ho sake toh apne liye koi kaam dekhlo aur agar mere liye bhi kuch ho toh batana.. ab aur ummid pe nahi jee sakta.. ghar ummido se nahi chalta paise chahiye ab."*

One of them said, *"tu chodh woh sab hum sab milkar kuch aur dekh lenge.. tu aunty ka khayal rakh hum nikalte hai."*

Taksh offered them to stay for sometime more but another explained, *"nahi yaar hume nikalna hai.. waise hi aate waqt bus waale ne der kar di ab jaane waali bus nahi chodh sakte.. mujhe aur Saket ko office join karni hai kal hi, Surbhi bhi bas aaj ki chutthi le paayi hai.."* Taksh now stares at all of them confusingly, all of them lowered their heads.

One of them briefs Taksh that they all had taken jobs, some are at stipend as interns, some are on full time jobs and a few are in part time, he stated, *"kya karte yaar.. hum afford nahi kar sakte the au delay aur kuch jo kar bhi rahe the tujhpe bharosa karke, unhone bhi ummid chodh di jab cargo China jaane ki news ayi."*

Taksh tells them it was okay and they chose the right thing, they all greeted goodbye and left.

Now a month had passed since Samrish's demise and Taksh and Pramila are all alone with the emptiness and void in the house and in their hearts, Taksh didn't know what to talk to at all, completely clueless, he took glances at his mother to check if she was crying again.

"Waise woh bujurg ko tu kaise jaanta hai jo uss din aye the gaadi mein?" Pramila questioned, breaking the haunting silence in the room. Taksh asked her why, she reverted, *"bas jaanne waale lage*

maano pehle mile ho mujhse.."

"Aapse? Kab?" Taksh squinched his face. Pramila sighed, trying remembering Rao. She stared at a picture on the wall that had Samrish and all his staff and workers, all of them standing together before the gate of their semiconductor factory, STL — SEMICONDUCTOR TECHNOLOGIES LIMITED. As she stared cluelessly at the picture, her expressioned changed and something struck her mind, just then we are taken back into a flashback in 1984.

Rakshit is looking around the house, workers are shifting furniture. Pramila is pregnant and with her baby bulge she is guiding the workers to arrange the furnitures properly. Samrish is seen running around taking care of everything, he sees Pramila standing and runs to her with a chair and offers her to sit. *"Tujhe supervisor banne kaun keh raha hai.. aisi halaat mein bistar se bhi nahi uthna hai tujhe."* Samrish asks the workers to install the bed in the bedroom immediately and then proceed with everything else.

"Main din bar bistar pe patient banke nahi padi reh sakti.. maa ban rahi hoon iska matlab ye nahi hai ki tum mere baap banoge.." Pramila and Samrish laugh out.

Samrish, then goes to Rakshit and asks the matter of the concern on his face. Rakshit explains, *"beta, hum bohot pair faila rahe hai, darr lag raha hai kahin chaadar choti na pad jaye."*

"aap iski fikar mat karo aap pair failao.. chaadar choti padne se pehle main nayi badi waali le aaunga." Samrish jokes.

"Itni acchi khaasi naukri chodhni nahi chahiye thi abhi.. bas kuch galat na ho ab.." Rakshit seems concerned.

"Aap itna kyun soch rahe ho.. waise bhi INTECH mein mujhe jitna bhi seekhna tha samajhna tha sab hogaya.. ab woh jagah mere liye nahi hai.. ab mujhe apna khudka plant lagana hai.. is desh mein ab Indian made semiconductor banane hai.. swadeshi semiconductors.." Samrish sounds ambitious as he speaks with sparkling eyes.

"Par beta tujhe toh maalum hi hai tere piyo ne aur maine kari thi koshish.. par kuch nahi hua..upar se abhi humara desh tayyar nahi hai aisi cheezo ke liye.. jahan 70% desh mein bijli hi nahi hai.. wahan ye factory lagana bewakoofi hai.. teri company INTECH ne bhi toh koshish ki thi na.. kya hua unka? Upar se sarkar ka kya bharosa kab palat jaye?"

Samrish assures him that whatever happened with others will not happen with them and they have spent 8 years into this now, Samrish tells him how he worked day and night so he can manage his job, family and STL all together.

"Jo karega soch samajh ke karna.. ab tera baccha hone wala hai bohot zimmedari aane waali hai tujhpe.. sarkaari baaton pe bharosa karna bewakoofi hoti hai.." Rakshit warns again.

"Aapne aaj tak mujhe sochne kahan diya kuch sab mujhse pehle aap hi samajh lete ho..aaj bhi aapki hi zarurat hai.. bas aap man jao fir jo thoda sa darr mujhe lag raha hai woh bhi bhaag jayega.." Samrish sits by him.

"Tu kar toh raha hai.. main kya hi karunga ab iss umar mein.." Rakshit tries to dodge him.

"Aap ko jo experience hai woh mere bohot kaam ayega.. mere toh baap ki jagah aap hi ho aur kisse madad maangu? Woh kar nahi paaye zindagi ne hume mauka diya hai.. bas aap maan jao fir sab thik hoga.." Samrish requests again.

"*aur tera woh scientist?*" Rakshit asks Samrish to talk to Rao about it as Rao has helped with initial capital and funding for operations.

"*Woh kya bolenge.. Udyan ji toh khud aapko bohot pasand karte hai unhone hi mujhe aapko convince karne ko kaha hai.*" Samrish tells Rakshit.

Rakshit pretends to give it a deep thought and utters, "*Mahina kitna dega mujhe?*"

Rakshit and Samrish laugh together, Pramila asks, "*aap dono chale jaoge toh main din bhar itne bade ghar mein kya karungi? Bhoote se baat?*"

"*Nahi Nahi.. apne gharwaalo se baat karne ki koi zarurat nahi hai.*" Samrish teases. "*Aur ye bada ghar kahan hai? Bada ghar toh hum lenge bohot jaldi..*" Samrish adds.

Udyan's car stops before the house, Udyan walks inside, calling out for Samrish. Pramila sighs, "*Kya faida hoga isse bade ghar ka jab rehna apko iss sautan scientist ke saath hi hai..*"

Udyan sees everyone, greets them all, asks Pramila about the kid and tells them that recently his daughter-in-law has also revealed her pregnancy to him. Rakshit jokes, "*fir toh agar apka beta humari beti ya apki beti humara beta hua toh hum rishtedaari ka haath badha lenge.*" All of them chuckle followed by Rao informing Samrish that he should come along with him to Delhi as the secretary of the PRESIDENT wants to brief him about the entire media event.

Rakshit inquires about it as it was very surprising for him when he hears about the President. Pramila is curious too, Rao and Samrish inform the other two that 7-8 years back they led the foundation for STL and the cabinet approved of it, the President was the CM of Punjab back then and he had allotted them 51 acres of land for the factory and he only took 1 rupees against it. And now when the factory is to be inaugurated and production is to begin in a few months he wants to do a media event praising his philanthropic and pro-industrialisation mindset. It will help him in his image building.

"He never leaves a chance to promote his good image." Samrish laughs.

"Uski qismat bhi kamaal hai pradhan mantri banna chahta tha.. seedha rashtrapati ban gaya.. isliye apni image ka kuch zyada hi dhyaan rakhta hai." Rao laughs as well.

"Koi na.. acche logo ke saath accha hota hai.. aur pradhan mantri bhi zarur ban jayenge.. main bhi rabb se bolungi ki ekdin unhe bhi pradhan mantri bana de." Pramila says innocently. Everyone else bursts out in laughter.

It is the day of the inauguration, Samrish is nervous and so is Rakshit. Rakshit is also a little emotional as he dreamt of this with Lokbhushan but Samrish was what destiny had conspired.

Samrish is busy attending politicians, media, Rao. Rao's son Srikanth and his wife, Sharmi had also come. Pramila and Sharmi were meeting for the first time but, they were the only ladies rather housewives at the event, they both became friends in a jiffy.

"Kya naam hai iska?" Sharmi asks about the child. *"Ladka hai ya ladki?"* She asks again.

"Ladka hai.. abhi naam rakha nahi hai..bas 44 din ka hi hai." Pramila tells her.

"Mera ladka hoga toh maine socha hai uska naam Taksh rakhungi..par tumhara hogaya aap rakhlo ye naam apko accha lage toh.." Sharmi says.

"Acha naam hai.. par fir aap kya rakhogi?" Pramila asks.

"Meri beti bhi toh ho sakti hai aur agar beta hua tab tak aap koi naam sochke bata dena.." Sharmi smiles.

"Atharv.. ye rakh lena apka beta hua toh.." Pramila tells Sharmi.

"Waise tumhe kuch samajh aya hai kya ki ye kis cheez ki factory hai?" Sharmi asks Pramila in a low voice.

"Nahi..bas itna maalum hai ye ki ye radio aur transistor aur telephone aur saare bijli se chalne waali cheezon ka dimag banane waale hai." Pramila replies.

"Batao aap inme bhi dimag hoga.. Kahin insaano se zyada na ho jaye..." Sharmi chuckles.

"Wohi.. dimaag banane ke karkhaane khul rahe hai.. duniya mein.. aaj machino ke fir insaano ke bhi khul jayenge kisi din.." Pramila shares her thought.

"Waise.. insaano ke dimaag ki factory khulna zaruri toh hai waise.. kaafi logo ko zarurat bhi hai..nahi?" Sharmi and Pramila laugh out loud, then hold themselves back to avoid unwanted attention from anybody around.

On the other hand, Srikanth and Samrish were also bonding nicely over future plans. Srikanth seemed very enthusiastic about STL and shared his wish to someday be able to do something similar. Samrish asked him if he did anything apart from assisting his father. Srikanth shook his head, Samrish offered him to work with Samrish and Rakshit at STL. Samrish also proposed the idea to Rao and after a little thinking, Rao agreed for it too. It was beneficial for Rao as his own son will be there to update him about all the workings of STL.

It is midnight, Pramila and Samrish wake Taksh up from sleep, it was his fifth birthday, they greet him, bring him his gifts and a cake to cut. Taksh wakes up with sleepy eyes and rubs his face.

"*Dadu?*" Taksh asks.

Samrish and Pramila call out for Rakshit. Samrish tells Pramila to stay with Taksh, he will go and bring Rakshit. He must be asleep. As Samrish is about to open the bedroom door, Rakshit barges in, panting. He informs Samrish, "*Factory se phone hai..jaldi neeche aa.*"

Samrish hears concern and tension in his voice, he rushes down to the telephone as he picks up the receiver and utters, "*Hello!*" Someone on the other side tells him something and his pace turns pale, he drops the receiver and cuts the call. He takes the car keys and drives off along with Rakshit. By the time Pramila comes down, they are gone.

CHAPTER SEVEN

Designed... Demolished

Samrish and Rakshit stood at the gate of their factory, surrounded by reporters and journalists, a few guards of the main gate and some other employees. Everybody stood helplessly staring at the massive building burn down to dust, there were occasional blasts amid the fire. By the time, fire brigade arrived and started the rescue, everything that was to be saved and everything that could be saved had already returned to nothingness in the form of ashes.

Reports were blabbering around as honeybees and Samrish and Rakshit were flowers to be pollinated for them. The fire fighters ask Samrish if he has any idea how many people were trapped inside. Samrish does not have any idea, he says *"mujhe nahi maalum par adhi raat ko koi hona toh nahi chahiye."*

One of the guards was overhearing their conversation and he revealed, *"Nahi sahab.. woh Srikanth sahab andar gaye the kuch 9 baje uske baad, unko bahar aate nahi dekha humne."* Listening this, the firefighters immediately send their men inside but Rakshit asked them to relax.

"Woh andar nahi honge.. aag lag chuki hai woh chale gaye honge.." Rakshit rubbed his face and eyes.*"Koi peeche gate pe tha kya?"*

"Nahi sahab." The guard looked down.

"*Srikanth nahi kar sakta hum pakka galat soch rahe hai.*" Samrish defends Srikanth.

"*Bilkul kar sakta hai akhir kar hai toh baap ka hi beta.. uss din us Udyan se teri ladai bhi uske samne hui thi.. woh apne baap ko beizzat hota dekh chup thodi rahega..*" Rakshit clarified.

A month and a half before the fire broke out, everybody was busy with their work when amidst the thudding sounds of the gigantic machines in operation, every ear present at the manufacturing plant heard the clamouring and hollering between Rao and Samrish. They were yelling at each other at the top of their lungs. Rakshit came out of her cabin, so did Srikanth. Rakshit gestured to the workers to stop the machines.

Rao and Samrish were indulged in an heated argument, Rao was convincing Samrish again to not bid for the equity of STL as if he bids he will be given preference over Rao but Rao wants to win the bid and commands Samrish to let go of it as Rao deserves the equity more than Samrish as he was the first one to believe in his vision and put his personal money. Samrish is defending him with gratitude for what Rao di but in the meantime, Rao has also made enough money because of STL and it wasn't possible with Samrish, the fight gets to a point where Samrish pushes Rao, Rao loses balance and almost falls, Samrish immediately apologises for his action and justifies it with impulse but Rao warns him to backup as he was about to snatch STL away from Samrish's grip. Rao saunters out after saying this. He also calls out for his son and asks him if he will go along but Srikanth respectfully denies. Samrish strolls back into his cabin and bangs the door.

The firefighters informed others that three bodies were found inside. Stretchers were sent inside. As the bodies were brought out, wallets, business cards, employee cards or anything else was being checked in the pockets. Two of the deceased were males and one female. Samrish failed to figure out as no woman worked at their factory.

"Isspe DL hai sahabji.. Koi Charan Bhullar hai..bichara puri tarah se jala bhi nahi hai bas upar ki body jal gayi.. usi wajah se jaan gay hogi.." One of the firefighter scream.

"Charan bhullar.. koi iss name ka apka staff tha kya?" another one asked Samrish and Rakshit. Rakshit denied and told them, they don't remember names of all the staff, they will have to check the registry. Now, Samrish was concerned if either of the two males was Srikanth.

The main gate guard intervened, *"Sahabji.. woh Srikanth ji ka driver aya tha Sharmi madam ko leke. Woh teeno andar hi the.. unki gaadi bahar nahi aayi."*

Samrish freezes at the spot and asks the rescuers to verify if two cars were parked and especially if any of it was blue in colour. One of the guys who took the stretchers inside confirmed that he saw two cars parked inside, one blue and another silver. Samrish looked at Rakshit, Rakshit regretted saying all of it about Srikanth. Samrish asks the guard to inform Udyan Rao. The guard rang the telephone but nobody picked up from the other side. By now, the police arrived at the spot and just after Rao came, he opened the door of his car and hopped out before it stopped. He saw the dead bodies of his son and daughter-in-law and broke down into tears. He wrapped his arms around Srikanth's burnt body and cried. The police constables held him back. Samrish holds him by his shoulders and consoles him as another blast took place inside the factory, the fire cloud rose as high as a 4 storey building.

"Ye andar dhamake kyun ho rahe hai? Andar radio ki jagah bamb

banate the kya?" The police officer asked.

"*Sir woh andar imported videshi machine hai unme gallium, germanium jaise elements use hote the IC develope karne mein.. aur bhi bohot sara chemical hota hai wohi aag se garam hokarr react kar rahe hai aur blast ho rahe hai...*" Rakshit explained the officer as he saw Samrish and Rao were not in the senses to talk anything.

"*Oh fikar waali bat ho hai jee.. aise toh pura mohali ud jayegaa..*" The police officer showed concern. "*Aur kisi ki koi bhi cheez ko nuksan hua toh bharpai apko karni hogi.*" The officer added.

"*Sir bharpai pehle humari kaun karega? Humara 50 60 cr ka samaan machine sab jal gaya..*" Rakshit muttered.

"*Apka nuksaan? Par ye toh sarkaari kaarkhaana hai?*" The officer asked. Rakshit looked at Samrish who looked around people and began thinking about how it all shattered in a moment that was built in years. The glimpses of the past began to float before his eyes.

The company that began its initial run with favours from people and politicians and with borrowed technical support outsourced from an American tech giant. But it did not take STL long to surpass the American technology and they became self sufficient in developing the chips completely, in-home. An indian semiconductor manufacturing plant that began production of 5 micron chips managed to produce 0.8 micron chips in a span of 4 years. In fact, 0.8 micron processors were the fastest and the most advanced processors in the entire world at that time. Things became so big that all the politicians and people who were involved in the creation of STL. It was becoming difficult for Samrish to deal with a new person everyday who will come and remind favours they did during or before setting up of STL. Samrish, Rakshit and Srikanth were indeed the people who were the reason behind it but

STL had its major shares allotted to the central government. So, on paper it belonged to the government. And, then 5 years later, in 1989, the central government declared that it would sell a part of their holdings to whoever wanted it. And a lot of people bid for it as it was backed by the name of the government that was trusted by everyone, the shares were eyed upon by a lot of people but Samrish won the bidding followed by Rao at the second number.

Rao on his side, earned a good name for him in ISRO and simultaneously became the chairman of the ISRO soon after the production began in STL. Now after all the technical upgrades and transformation of STL which was only possible because of Rakshit and his experience. now, Rao was eyeing to become the owner of STL. He would often suggest to Samrish in other words how he has expansion plans for STL and wanted Samrish to withdraw his bid so, he can get possession of all the major stake holding in STL. It was also the very reason for the clash and quarrel between Samrish and Rao. There was no way Samrish was letting STL become anyone else's.

Samrish and Srikant were now best friends and have bonded well over time. Srikanth had always worked under his father assisting him in his projects and rao never let him led a project but Samrish used to handover multiple projects to Srikanth and would trust him even at any moments, when Srikanth doubted himself. These reasons made Samrish very dear to Srikanth. Srikanth would handle and manage the entire operation of STL, Rakshit took care of research and development and Samrish kept manufacturing and technology for his shoulders. Rao used to get involved in the operation and would often nose into the deals and all buut never crossed his lines until he was designated as the ISRO chairman. After that, something changed and he picked up god complex.

Samrish and Srikanth redirected multiple government deals and dozens of private ones. But the pace at which STL was growing was concerning for the other tech giants, and after STL, multiple companies began trailing the path of STL but failed to manufacture chips below 2 microns. After STL successfully tested its 0.8 micro processors, they were overbooked with orders. ISRO was lagging behind during that phase, ISRO needed a reliable technology, discovery, anything at all to prove its mettle and that was how Rao decided to acquire STL under ISRO. He wanted Srikanth to lead STL but Srikanth never intended anything as such against his best friend, Samrish.

Around 2 months before the night of the fire, Srikanth stops his car, gets down with a few files and heads inside the factory, he walks through the narrow passage between the machines towards the cabin of Samrish, he stops at the door, knocks it. Samrish calls him in, *"knock toh mat kiya kar bhai.."*

Srikanth sits, Rakshit was also sitting on one of the chairs, smoking. Srikanth shows him the file of papers he carried and explains how their 0.8 micron processors were ground breaking technology on the face of earth and they must protect it before somebody else develops it too. Samrish and Rakshit tried to consume what he said but it was out of their mental abilities, *"Are seedha bolna kya karna hai?"* Samrish questions.

"hume patents file karne honge to protect our intellectual property.. aur ekbar patents grant hogaye toh duniya mein koi aur humari technology use karke ye chips nahi bana payega.. aur agar bana bhi lega toh hume royalty aur credits dene honge." Srikanth looks at both of Samrish and Rakshit's faces who were all ears to the plan.

"Toh karwa lete hai.. kisse baat karni hogi batao main phone karta hoon." Rakshit picks up the telephone receiver. Srikanth stops him and explains how patents can't be filed with referals and contacts, they needed to follow the procedure as it was designed. Rakshit

again suggested to offer some bribe and get patents immediately but Srikant cuts him down again. Eventually all of them fill up the forms, file the request to grant them technology patents.

One more addition to their happy days, the patents were granted and Srikanth, Samrish and Rakshit were asked to appear for a personal invigilation round where, the invigilators would grant or reject their requested patents. Unfortunately, the date of the invigilation just three days when the fire broke out.

Back again at the night of the fire, we see, the fire was put out, the fire brigade was preparing to leave from the location, the entire building structure of the factory was burnt black. Samrish, Rakshit and Rao were being questioned by the police when one of the constables came and whispered something in the ears of the interrogating officer, he signalled other policemen and all circled around Samrish, Rakshit and Rao. The officer then handcuffed Rao and asked him to cooperate while they arrest him for conspiring and ordering the fire to break out. Rao, silently gets into the police car. Rakshit looked at Rao and uttered, "*Kaise admi hai aap.. apni zidd ke aage apne bete bahu ko hi marwa diya?*" Samrish could not believe it either but he was devasted and disturbed enough by the loss of his factory and everything else that he spent his life to build upon.

Samrish recalled his last interaction with Srikanth in the morning when he invited Srikanth, Sharmi and Ishu, their daughter for the birthday of Taksh. Rakshit asked Srikanth to bring along the patent files as it was better to be kept at home. Srikanth agreed to the idea and said, "*Haan.. main raatko aane se pehle file lete hue aunga..*"

Isha was whinning, she was down with fever. Srikanth and Sharmi were sitting beside her bed, cheering her up when Sharmi suggested, "*Aap ho aao bhaiya bhabhi ke ghar se.. mera aisi halat mein jaana sahi nahi hoga..main iske paas ruk jaati hoon.*"

"*Nah, main bhi rukunga.. Samrish samajh jayega baad mein.*" Srikanth offers to stay too, followed by half an hour long discussion, Sharmi suggested, he goes and delivers the files, he was talking about in the evening. Srikanth recalled the patent files.

By now, Isha was asleep and her fever was also down to normal levels after medicines. Srikant recalled the file was at the office only. Sharmi asked him to go and get it from the office and then deliver it to Samrish and also deliver the gift they got for Taksh. Srikanth asked Sharmi to come along and they will just give the gift and file and will come back home immediately after that.

"*Acha thikhai aap file leke aaiye tab tak iski neend bhi gehri ho jayegi...fir chalte hai.*" Sharmi asked him to get the files from the factory. Srikanth leaves for the factory, after sometime, Sharmi finds Isha sleeping, all tucked in and Srikanth was taking longer than he should, she asked one of the drivers to drive her to STL and she leaves for the factory too.

Pramila was in the kitchen, Taksh was on the sofa doing his homework, Samrish walks inside the house after greeting the lawyer, goodnight. Pramila calls him to her and asks, "*Ho gaya.. ab jaane dete hai.. bhagwan ki marzi ke aage kya hi kar sakte hai hum?*"

Samrish does not react, Pramila sighs and asks Samrish to call Taksh and Rakshit for dinner. Samrish calls out Taksh and pushes the door open and walks into Rakshit's room. "*Khana khaa lijiye aake—*" Samrish is petrified as he sees the Rakshit hanging lifelessly through the fan.

CHAPTER EIGHT

Last Lap to go

A couple of years have passed after Rakshit's death. Samrish is seen bouncing around government offices seeking help to restablish STL but all his efforts were in vain. The kind of capital required to resume operations was not a matter of any one of the ministeries, nor was the high command keen on spending anything. Disappointment to Samrish has become like insulin to the diabetic; willingly or unwillingly, a dose or two were to be taken everyday.

Pramila would see her husband leaving for work with an upset face and would see her coming back home in the evening with an even more upset, lowered, dull face. It seemed as Samrish's new job was paying him more grief in salary instead of money. Throughout the weeks, he would grind as a product manager at BHEL and in the weekends Samrish would go on a spree to different government offices at all levels. Every now and then, Samrish would be approached by the high command to give up his plans to revive the STL and rather sell it off to some government backed organisation like DRDO or ISRO.

Thankfully Samrish was making enough money through his job to keep his family financially-abled, Pramila would be raising Taksh alone as after Rakshit, Samrish stopped talking to his family and would only stay home or hardly a couple of hours. When Pramila was informed about the deal to sell STL, Pramila began convincing Samrish to do it and move on in life. Samrish was yet not ready.

On the other side, Rao was released from custody as a few phone calls from some higher ranks were made and the police shut the case and released Rao.

Now, we see Rao is sitting in the house, having his evening drink, Isha was asleep. Isha's nanny comes and asks Rao if she could leave as all her work for the day was done. Rao nods his head and allows her to leave. As Rao and Isha are alone, a white car comes into the compound of the house and stops right before thr main entrance. Rao walks out and finds it was one of his friends from the union ministries.

"Kaafi logo ko naraaz kiya hua hai tumne, Rao. Jaldi kuch karo warna ab Mamla main bhi nahi sambhal paunga.." Rao's friend expresses.

"I'm not ready for it now.. mujhse ye nahi hoga.. main toh balki kahunga.. ki government ko STL firse setup karna chahiye... Aane Wale INDIA ki ye woh sidi hai jo is desh ko sabse upar le jayegi.." RAO asks his friend to come inside.

They both walk inside the house and take a seat, *"Humari sarkar toh tayyar hai.. aap ekbar Samrish se baat karo.. ki woh STL apko bech de... iske baad jaisa aap kahoge waise hi sab hoga."* Rao' friend asks for a drink.

"Mera beta...Bahu...dono cheen gaye... STL cheente huye...ab meri poti ke liye mera yahan rehna bohot zaruri hai.. baat toh aap hi kar sakte ho usse." Rao suggests.

"Rao sahab.. baat aisi hai ki aap pe jo charge hataye gaye hai STL jalwane ke... woh.. kabhi bhi dobara lag sakte hai... kya hai na..aaj kal bohot tarah ke activis agaye hai.." He sips his drink.

"Activists." Rao corrects him.

"apko toh pata hi hai...fir kyun bacchi ko akele chodhke jail jana chahte hai? Samrish se baat kariye.. use boliye ki factory ISRO ko de de." The tone of his friend turns more commanding.

He finishes his drink and takes leave, Rao didn't get up from his seat nor did he greet him goodbye. Rao looks at his family's photo and sighs, remorsefully.

A few days later, Samrish and Rao cross paths at the office of the MeitY [MINISTRY OF ELECTRONICS AND INFORMATION TECHNOLOGY.]

Samrish started glowering at Rao when he saw him, he ignored him as much as he could and walked past him that is when Rao calls him, Samrish didn't stop but a few more calls by Rao and Samrish stopped walking and strided towards Rao but he could not say anything as words fumbled insides his mouth, he was so angry, he just kept looking at him. Rao asks him to listen to him once.

Rao and Samrish are sitting on opposite ends of a table. A waiter comes and plonks two cups of tea before them. Rao inquires about Taksh, Samrish asks him to come straight to the point and not waste his time. Rao exhales deeply, as Rao began to convince Samrish to sell STL, Samrish stops him midway and speaks, *"Accha matlab jab high command se nahi hua toh unhone apne sabse brilliant officer ko bheja hai?"*

Before Rao could counter it, Samrish added, *"ek aur baat.. STL toh humesha se majorly government ke under hi thi.. abhi tak dilution toh hua nahi hai...fir mujhe manane ki itni zarurat kyun hai?"*

"Kyunki Major stakeholder operations mein apni chala sakta hai par

decisions like company bandh karna, bechna ya aisa sab.. isme sabki permission chahiye hoti hai... aur Government wants to take STL under ISRO." Rao explains.

"Government ya fir aap? ISRO toh.." Samrish chuckles and gets up from his seat and continues, *"jab police apko apne hi bete ke murder ke liye le gayi.. toh mujhe tab bhi laga ki chahe kuch bhi ho Rao Sahab apne bete ko thodi marenge... ho hi nahi sakta hai unhone ye aag lagwai..lekin ab Lag raha hai...aap apni baat manwaane ke liye kuch bhi kar sakte ho... koi nahi.. ekdin jawab apko bhi dene padenge... aur STL agar khulega toh jaise pehle tha waisa hi khulega warna band hi sahi."* Samrish began to walk.

"Maine bas log bheje the... Plan high command ka hi tha.." Rao defends.

Samrish turns around, pounds his palms on the table, *"aur High command ko kisne convince kiya tha to take over STL?"*

Rao sits wordless, Samrish walks off.

A week or two after Rao met Samrish, Samrish was arrested from his office for accepting bribes from and leaking company's confidential information to the competitors.

Samrish knew what was happening, he didn't even resist. He assumed Rao to be doing it. As Samrish was taken into custody, inside the interrogation room, the interrogation officer begins to threaten Samrish to agree to the government and let go of STL; otherwise it would be years that he will have to spend in jail.

Pramila along with Taksh has come to the police station and pleads the police to let her meet Samrish but they keep her waiting for hours before Samrish is allowed to meet his family that too after one of the constables took Taksh away from Pramila. Pramila resisted but was overpowered by other officers, the interrogating officer again asks Pramila to convince her husband to let go of STL else, he looks towards the gate from where Taksh walked off with a constables who offered him toffees and candies.

Pramila runs inside the interrogation chamber and sees Samrish and just sits down and holds his legs and cries heart-wrenchingly to give in to the demands of the police else Taksh was taken somewhere and if Samrish doesn't comply, they may not see Taksh again. Samrish got up and was just about to scream to his loudest but then sat back and his face turned blue from red. He calls for the officer and tells him to let his family alone, he was ready to do whatever was demanded.

Sometime later, Rao comes there and present some papers to Samrish and requests him to sign. Rao was not looking up in shame but only he knew how helpless he was and if he didn't do what was told he'd end up at rhe same position as Samrish was sitting.

"Le toh Liya..par STL mere bina kabhi nahi chalegi... Dekh lena.." Samrish sobs like a kid as he said this while signing the documents.

"Jo tumhare hisse ki value hai.. woh paise tumhe gold bonds mein mil jayenge..." Rao tells Samrish.

"Rakh lo..woh bhi...nahi chahiye mujhe iske paise.." Samrish keeps the pen down and slides the papers to Rao.

After that day, Samrish took up a supervisor's job in a small factory that paid him just enough to survive. Samrish was also offered the money a number of times but he didn't accept it. They had to sell their house and shift to a rather smaller place but Samrish slowly began to focus on his work and his family and stopped thinking about STL. There will be news about reviving STL every now and then but it hardly mattered to Samrish.

Time passed and things changed but STL couldn't be revived. On the other side, Taksh was a teenage now, he was appearing for his boards and Samrish like any other father was suggesting him to choose a career and go for Doctor or C.A. but Taksh had other plans. When Taksh expressed his wish to study engineering and take back all that was snatched from his father, Samrish commands him to think straight and not lose his grip over life, he asks him to choose a better life and a different path else semiconductors have ruined his and his father's life and will not hesitate to ruin his son, Taksh's life too. Taksh was adamant in the beginning, Pramila tried convincing Samrish as well but when Samrish didn't agree, like an obedient son, Taksh agreed to study whatever his father thought was best for him but just requests his father to allow him to go and study in Delhi as Mohali didn't offer quality education.

Samrish and Pramila were coming back from the bus stand after they see-off Taksh. As they approached home, a postman stood at their gate. On inquiring, he handed them an envelope that had a government seal on it. Samrish opens it and as he kept reading It, his eyes sparkled in glee and his face changed, Pramila was excited to see such happiness on Samrish's face. She questions him about the content of the letter.

Samrish then reveals, the current government has asked him to pay a visit as they wanted to discuss something regarding a new semiconductor plant and wanted Samrish to lead it. Pramila then saw Samrish's face turning colourless again. Samrish told her, *"Kya fayda? Chodho..sala fir koi aake mere haqq ka le jayega aur nahi padhna mujhe ye politics ke lafde mein.."* Samrish carelessly throws the letter and walks in. Pramila picks it up and spends some days just trying to convince Samrish to at least go once. Samrish was hesitant and didn't want his past to repeat again. But in a few days, the tempting thought of being able to do what he loves was luring him, so he eventually decides to appear for the meeting.

Samrish came back home after 2 days, Pramila was happy to see him return home with a happy face after almost a decade. Samrish was jumping around in joy as he told how he got a chance to meet the PM of the country, he went on to praise the PM and his behaviour, he further tells her how, a man on the seat of the PM requested Samrish to lead the venture as everything will be as per Samrish would suggest.

Samrish then sounded a little low when he expressed grief that this time, he'd be all alone as Rakshit will no be there to guide him nor was his best friend Srikanth who would take care of everything. Samrish told Pramila that some of the people in the meeting were offering him to offer Rao to join him for the venture as Rao had taken early retirement from his career and was now, sitting idle at home with his grandchild.

Pramila asks Samrish to go and talk to Rao once but Samrish told her that he is not interested in falling for another trickery of Rao and wanted to keep a distance as far as he could from the cunning old man. Soon, things began as they should, Samrish quit his job and focused on the new plant setup and researched about the newer technologies that had developed in the last years when he wasn't around.

It was an important day for Samrish, the factory land was to be allotted and the machinery was to be bought today, Samrish and Pramila had gone to a temple and as they came back, the newspaper boy delivered the paper for the day, Samrish picks it up and asks the newspaper boy to get off from his cycle and keep the paper in a decent manner.

"*Khud jaake le aya karo uncle.. itna time nahi hai mere pe..*" He cycled away.

Samrish was waiting for his tea as he unfolded the newspaper. The front page was —

"*INDIA SUCCESSFULLY PERFORMS ITS NUCLEAR TESTING...*"

Realisations and Rectifications

"Dekh lijiye sir agar mumkin ho.. please sir.." Samrish pleads as he stands before his boss.

This is the same job Samrish quit but was begging to get it back as once again, things fell off the target. As hi boss asks him to leave, he walks out recalling the incidents in the last few days.

After the news of the successful nuclear testing came out, India celebrated and for the first time Samrish felt confident about his dream as he saw the dynamic moves of the current government. All his hesitation faded away after this, he was assured that nothing can hurdle his way this time but soon things came collapsing down upon him when the scheduled plans begun to being postponed yet again.

The news channels were hollering about the global criticism that India was facing due to such a drastic step. America had imposed sanctions on India and India was denied trade at the world stage. The economy collapsed, the YoY growth went negative, the government was facing internal criticism by the opposition parties and some so-called intellectuals. So in such chaos, it was obvious and evident that the government was not at a position to take another risky call that too with extreme shortage of government funds. The year was so harsh on India that India was lacking funds to import the basic necessities, the foreign reserves were down to zero and the only thing that let India survive was intervention of the IMF and the foreign reserves were put back by the NRIs who used to send money home. The condition was as critical as one could imagine.

From India's journey to prove itself as a nuclear superpower to being denied the status of so, by western powers and then the imposed sanctions and how it pushed India decades back in time and then just at the verge of an economic collapse, IMF offered loans and slowly India stood back on its feet, the entire journey is as similar to a cactus that was planted in a mangrove forest.

We all have heard of cactus, a plant that needs less to extremely less water to grow and thrive, but if you take it from a droughted region and plant it back in swampy wet region, you'd see, the plant will show you signs of happy growth, vibrancing colour but then all of a sudden, the wet soil will infect the roots of the cactus and in no time the roots will rot away that will kill the plant as fast as it showed false signs of thriving growth. The only way to solve such a cactus is to plant it back to the place it belongs, for a few things in the universe are not to be adapted but accepted. And in this story: India is the cactus.

Anyway, so yes, the semiconductor dreams of India shattered once again but what shattered more that day, was Samrish. Samrish shattered like a broken ceramic vase that chipped and splintered into tiny pieces and kintsugi was the only option that could save him but unfortunately, the required lacquer and gold was way beyond unaffordable for the little vase.

After that day, Samrish never talked about it, he didn't discuss anything with his wife but Pramila guessed his state and didn't bother him either. Samrish has wasted a large chunk of his savings and only an urgent permanent job could help his family from being there on the streets. Pramila never saw Samrish smile, past that. But Pramila's hopes to see the old Samrish demolished when Samrish found out Taksh lying about his studies in the field of commerce where in reality he was pursuing engineering in micro technology. Samrish would have ripped Taksh's skin off but his expectations from life and people were down to minus one. Pramila realised her husband was just a breathing body of flesh, bones and blood, he was barely alive anymore.

And soon after that, after Taksh's 1st year of college, Samrish was becoming more prone to infections and would catch fever and cold easily. Samrish soon got diagnosed with Aplastic anaemia and he kept it under the nose for years until things worsened and became untreatable. Perhaps, his blood cells gave up on him too when his mind and conscience lost their purpose to live. Samrish swallowed death, day by day in small doses until the day he could actually stop breathing.

This government was perhaps the first one that actually took major steps to push India forward at world charts, not just through nuclear testing, but also by focusing on India's previous failure in the semiconductor industry, Infrastructure development, inviting foreign corporations and efficient trade with other countries but good things barely last and after the 1998 sanctions imposition, the government was blamed and India fell back into a pit of political instability as well.

And in 1998 with India becoming a nuclear power, Samrish's story came to its very end. Samrish refrained from anything and everything, he continued working as a small time employee for a couple of years more then eventually his dying body gave up and his health worsened and worsened and worsened and one day, it was over...

Now coming back to the present, it has been few months since Samrish died, Taksh was in a similar state to what his father was after the 1989 factory shut down. He felt like it was the end of his world too but Taksh's one last hit was still pending. A more gruesome wound was yet to come Taksh's way. Albeit! It was still years away from him.

After Samrish's death Taksh appeared for multiple job interviews but would fail miserably. Pramila would spend most of her days sitting idle staring at Samrish's picture into oblivion.

On the other side, Rao was trying his best, he was utilising all his contacts to get Taksh what the entire Dabral family deserved. But Rao was not as important for anybody to be able to pull off what he was aiming for. Meanwhile, he meets his old friend, he is the same politician cum ex-minister who has threatened Rao to convince Samrish to let go of STL back in the 1990s.

Rao explains the situation to him and asks him to intervene and see if anything at all could be done for now, the world was a witness how semiconductors were shaping the new age technology and the industry was at a J curve, India must jump into it. The minister revealed that some of the foreign competitors of INTEK are actually willing to put a factory and that's the best he could have done for Taksh that too only for the sake of Rao.

But immediately, he chuckles and mock about it and shouts at Rao for his audacity to come to seek help from him and asks him to leave. "*Manna padega Rao sahab.....besharam hone ki agar koi hadd hoti toh aap toh us hadd ki bhi hadd paar kar gaye ho..*"

Rao leaves the place and sits in his car recalling events from the past when this minister and Rao had broiling battle of words because when Rao got Samrish to let go of his stakes in STL, Rao was also supposed to get the technology patents from Samrish for the 0.8 micron semiconductor nanochips. The entire MeitY was upset about the matter as the patent and that technology blueprint was the main reason to accquire STL without that STL had to develop all of it again.

Rao tried his best to explain to them that it is because they hurried in burning up the place and did it before the personal interview round was scheduled for the patent granting. And this blunder gave Samrish a winning hand as Rakshit killed himself and Rao's son Srikanth was killed in the fire, Samrish was the only one alive and he appeared for the P.I. and due to STL being burnt down he asked for the patent to be granted under his name and not STL. So when they forced him to let go of STL, the patents didn't belong to STL but Samrish. It was Samrish's intellectual property and couldn't be taken away like anything.

It was 2007 and few foreign companies who had planned their semiconductor ventures in India were backing off as India lacked the desired Infrastructure, power source and whatnot! So just on the basis of cheap and affordable manpower, it was not wise to set up the foundation stone of an entire new industry with such high risk.

Meanwhile, the other countries already involved in the semiconductor manufacturing were now way ahead of what India could have done years ago but to technological disappointment of the world, no other nation was even near the chip that Samrish and STL had developed 20 years ago from that time.

By now, Taksh has taken a job in the RnD department of one of the leading technology companies. Taksh and Pramila were moving on from Samrish's demise. And one usual evening, Rao came to pay a visit to Taksh in Mohali. Taksh greeted him as warmly as he always did, he inquired about Isha. Pramila was now aware who Rao was and she had all the past events in mind, she had recalled it all but Rao appeared weak and helpless but Pramila could still not trust the man. Rao asked Taksh to accompany him to somewhere he wanted to go. Pramila was asking Taksh not to but without letting Pramila complete, Taksh followed him out. Pramila begun to regret and got worried for she couldn't trust Rao with her son now, after what he did to her husband.

On this side, Rao took Taksh to STL. *"Dabral Sahab, apko pata hai ye kya hai?"* Rao asked.

"Haan... ek time pe Papa ne shuru ki thi.." Taksh was staring at the board.

"Fir kya hua kuch pata hai?" Rao asked again.

"Papa ne shuru ki thi...fir ek accident mein puri factory jal gayi aur end mein Papa ko ye bech dena pada... dadu bhi guzar gaye the toh papa ki himmat nahi hui ki woh akele fir se sab khada kar sake.." Taksh spilled all that he knew.

"Kahani bas itni si nahi hai.." Rao begins.

"Rehne dijiye sir... kuch cheezein itni si hi rehni chahiye.." Taksh stops him

"Ye batana zaruri hai..mere liye.... aur janna.. tere li—" Rao is cut again.

"Aap jo batana chahte ho mujhe pata hai.. rehne dijiye...fayda nahi hai unn gade murdo ko nikalke.. jo jawaab se zyada sawaal de jaye.. unhe kabr mein hi rehne dijiye.. saalo beet gaye.. Papa bhi ab nahi rahe.. ab main bhi apse bair rakh ke kya karlunga? " Taksh says.

Rao is startled at this, of course, he had no idea that Pramila had already told Taksh about things the same day Samrish died and Pramila asked about Rao, as she was looking into Samrish and STL inauguration picture, Rao was in the picture and that reminded her of all, she didn't waste any time to warn Taksh against Rao.

Rao silently looks at Taksh and lits a cigarette, "*Aur mera toh koi beta bhi nahi hai jisse tu khandani dushmani nikaale..*" He laughs a little, then continues, "*Lekin beta, maine kabhi bhi tera bura nahi cha—*" Taksh stops him again.

"*Jaane dijiye sir.. ye baat nahi karte hai ab...kahin nahi pahochenge...hum..*" Taksh tells him again, Rao is just astonished to see Taksh sound so mature. "*Waise aapne cigarette kab chalu kiya?*" Taksh asks.

Rao takes a puff, "*shuru toh 16 ki umar mein kiya tha par pehle...apne baap ke darr se chodh di...fir biwi baccho ke wajah se...aur fir Isha ki wajh se... Ab kya hai akele rehta hoon.. toh kabhi kabhi pee leta hoon..*"

"*Isha?*" Taksh questions.

"*... usko bhi toh yehi lagta hai ki uske maa baap ko maine hi mara hai...usse nahi raha gaya... bolke gayi hai ki mere marne pe bhi nahi ayegi..*" Rao throws the cigarette and stomps it down. "*Socha prayaschit ki toh umar nikal gayi.. toh sach hi bol leta hoon shayad kuch halka lagne lage..*" Rao adds again.

"*Toh laga halka..?*" Taksh questions him.

"*Pura khaali..ekdum khokla lagne laga hai..*" Rao bursts down into tears as he utters this. Taksh was looking at somebody cry like that for the 2nd time in his life, first was his father who weeped like Rao after Rakshit's death.

Rao and Taksh are back home, Pramila is not happy to see Rao coming again and she decides to ask him not to interfere in their lives further but Rao with folded hands apologises for whatever he caused. Pramila didn't accept his apology and went inside. Taksh asked him about Isha and Rao told him about Isha being in Jaipur.

"Jaipur mohali se kitni dur hai?" Taksh asks.

"Bohot?" Rao says.

"Maa..main abhi ata hoon..." Taksh informs Pramila and rushes out.

"gadi le ja..." Rao offers his car keys

"Le jaunga...lekin jab apni khareedunga..." Taksh runs back inside.

"Kya hua ab? Kya chahiye?" Pramila asks while Taksh is looking around for something.. *"bol toh kya chahiye? Main dhundh deti hoon.."* Pramila asks again.

Taksh breathes out and asks, *"woh sketchbook kahan hai Papa ki?"* Pramila gives it to him and Taksh runs out.

Taksh and Isha are sitting by a bench at a lakeside, there's enough gap between them, Taksh asks her to come back but Isha refuses. Taksh requests her a number of times more but all in vain.

"Mere ghar Chalegi?" Taksh asks.

"Aur bolega kya ghar pe?" Isha questions back.

"Pehle tujhe bol lu.. fir ghar pe bol dunga.." Taksh now slides near her.

"*Kya?*" Isha asks, confusingly.

Taksh turns towards Isha, facing her, brings out his sketchbook and shows it to Isha. Isha flips the pages and sees incomplete drawings. She doesn't understand it and asks Taksh again, "*Ye kya hai?*"

"*Ab dekh humare khaandani kangan toh rahe nahi...tere dada ki meharbaani se...*" Taksh and Isha both giggle a little at the joke, then Taksh continues, "*Bas ye aadhi sketch waali kitab bachi hai..*"

They both begin to flip pages and Taksh keeps explaining all the pictures —The first incomplete picture was of Samrish, Lokbhushan and Samrish's mother but she died during the Influenza epidemic in India and the picture couldn't be completed.

The second page was a drawing of Samrish, Lokbhushan and Rakshit but in that drawing, Lokbhushan wasn't complete as Lokbhushan left Samrish with Rakshit.

The third one was Samrish, Pramila, Taksh and Rakshit.. and in this, Rakshit was missing. The next page was empty.

Taksh kept explaining to Isha the reasons of all that and when they both reached the empty page, Taksh held Isha and warmly hugged her, "*Iss me saare sketch adhure hai... Mere saath iss kitaab ki pehli puri sketch banayegi?.. Tu, Main aur Maa.*"

Isha looks at Taksh with sparkling eyes and leans her head on his shoulder, they sit there without any movement, in silence. The sun changed its colour to orange, yellow, then more orange and clandestinely scuttled and submerged into the lake as Taksh and Isha leaned their heads on each other, euphorically imagining their own utopia.

CHAPTER TEN

Holler of the Hero

It was the summer of 2012; The entire northern belt of India was broiling; The heatwaves were at their extreme; the temperature was breaking records, everyday. Heat strokes, Sun strokes are becoming a daily problem now. The world was beginning to experience the initial climatic changes due to global warming. Meanwhile, a rumour about the 'Ultimate Apocalypse'; the end of the world was already circulating around the air. People were in panic, every news article, every news channel was broadcasting their own theory about it.

Pramila was recently back home after her appendix removal surgery. She has formed a gang of other colony aunties and all of them used to go out for morning and evening walks together and would patrol around the area, gossiping about everything while accepting, cherishing and embracing their coming old age.

Imran was now a ward councilor of a locality in New Delhi, he contested the elections in 2010 and won with adequate margins. The area was abounded with college hostels, PGs, etc. Being involved in college politics, he was a known name in the area and that really helped him during in the win.

Harman was now running his own electronics shop is Gaffar Market, coolers were his hero products those days. He was to be married the coming year in an arranged marriage setting. Harman and Taksh were still friends but not as much friends as they used to be. Imran and Harman and Taksh all met once or twice a year now; they talked about life and everything but the warmth they shared was not around anymore.

Taksh and Isha are married now; Taksh is working at HCTL — A market giant in industrial and commercial technology development. Taksh was not sure if this is what he wanted to do but was sure it was all he wanted to achieve in life — a stable family life.

And away from all of this, Rao lived alone. Isha never went to see him again, Taksh would often go and see him but because of Isha Rao never visited Taksh to make sure Isha is not uncomfortable because of him. He occasionally tried to make calls to her but Isha was happy in her life with Taksh and Pramila. They were soon to be parents, everything was good, in fact, great except for the fact that Taksh was headed to take another bullet to his chest.

And STL, as Samrish said STL never saw the glory that it saw during the reign of Samrish, Srikanth and Rakshit. The government tried reviving STL, a number of times but never could. Eventually, STL was converted into a laboratory from a manufacturing factory of semiconductor chips, ICs, motherboards, semi-insulators, microchips, etc.

A year ago before the 2014 elections in India, the then government had announced a budget of ? 39000 Crores to be allotted to set up the semiconductor industry in India. Taksh was lusting for the news but was willing to take another risk to quit everything and pursue it madly so he came up with another way. As he worked in a technology company, he prepared a presentation and presented it to his bosses and managed to bring them to an agreement to put money in the upcoming bidding for the semiconductor plant.

News about India rectifying its past mistakes was broadcasted around, and the exponentially growing market was about to grow further. All the midcap and bigcap corporations jumped into the bidding to get the elephantine budget for their company. Taksh's bosses put in their bid too but a few months later, one after the after, most of the companies were backing off or clearing their names off the bidding list. HCTL did nothing different, Taksh tried more than he could to stop them from taking that decision but it just didn't work out. Taksh was informed that some internal sources have confirmed the Government being biased towards INTEK and other biggies like JP group, HSMC, and IBM all had to back off after being shown no interest towards them. Taksh was not really affected this time and didn't let this event affect him majorly.

To everyone's surprise, even INTEK backed off and never really spoke about its reasons. Conspiracies claim that it was just another hoax strategy by the then government to defend its failures in semiconductors as national and international media was criticizing their past decisions that led to India's wasted potential in that field. Moreover, elections were around the corner, just a year away so the news was broadcasted and hyped with propaganda to save their seats.

Elections happened and so did what was expected: the government changed. The country was now being run by a visionary leader and his capable, responsible cabinet of ministers. Necessary actions are to be taken to revive the semiconductor industry in India, this government brought some much-delayed policies back to life and pushed India towards the ladders of progress, development, and growth.

A year later in 2014, Taksh received a letter; letter from STL. Everyone in the family was unsure of their reactions; Pramila was skeptic and hesitant to let Taksh put his hands again in that pit. She asked her to ignore the letter. Taksh was still staring at the envelope, Isha told him to go through it.

The letter had 3 motives, it started with gratitude towards Taksh's father and his grandfather for their contribution towards India's growth but for whatever reason it didn't happen, they must be given their due credits. The second part was about revival plans of STL and government and ministries backing it and all such information was provided. The letter also stated how the new government has plans to set up semiconductor plants and focus on the Make in India movement so the nation becomes self-sufficient by reducing imports. The third part of the letter was an invitation for Taksh. It was a scheduled appointment with the then, MeitY officers and STL managing director of that time. The letter also had an open job offer for Taksh.

Taksh didn't tell Pramila about it. Isha was aware of Taksh's thoughts but she didn't interfere and let him free to choose what he wants. Taksh being the son of Samrish and grandson of Lokbhushan, the Dabral DNA was what he was made up of too. He couldn't hold himself for long and left for STL.

Though it was founded by his father, Taksh had never seen the property from inside. It was the first time Taksh saw it all with his own eyes. As he approached the cabin that once belonged to his father, there were a number of people already waiting for him.

The meeting had just one known face, of Sanath. Everyone in the meeting began praising him and his family... but before Taksh could have a mouthful of such praises, the topic of the meeting shifted to the technology patents of his father. Each of them was just interested in it and asked Taksh about the patent in their own words. Taksh was now able to see the real picture. Everybody began telling him the importance of those patented technology algorithms. They even offered him a job as a vice-chairman of STL if he offered to trade the patent in return.

It didn't take much time before Taksh realised the entire show was put up not for him but the patent that belonged to his father. Taksh was somewhat aware of the importance of the file as it had algorithms to achieve 0.8 micron chips whereas the world was still far behind that number. Whereas his father had it decades back. Even today, people were just after that and all the attention and applaud that was being served to Taksh was not his but for that file.

To utmost unfortune, the meeting made Taksh realise why his father never gave the patents to Taksh when he asked for it. Samrish knew his son was being fooled and everyone was just after his lifetime's hard work. Taksh decided to run back home, he excused himself and walked out and didn't go back to the cabin.

He cried, hollered, sobbed, whined, wept and missed his father like never before. He wanted to hold him and hug, he missed how his father fondled his hair when he pretended to be asleep. He regretted not being with his father in his last moments.

He felt like running away somewhere, somewhere far away. He felt weak, stupid and incapable. He wanted to run away, he took a ride to the bus stand and booked a bus ticket for Manali. He sat there in the bus staring into oblivion outside, recalling all that happened in his life. The bus driver started the engine and slowly drove away.

Isha gave birth to a little girl, Pramila was playing with her kid, Harman and Imran were present there as well. Isha looked at the door waiting for Taksh but the door stood still like a wall between two distinct worlds, the door seemed like a formidable barrier, thick and imposing, crossing it was only possible by facing one's fears and Taksh was on the other side of that wall.

To cross that wall, one had to face their insecurities, failures and show extreme courage, the courage that Taksh lacked, the fear of failure like his father and grandfather who escaped from their failures. Taksh did the same but that one moment, that one moment when he hopped down from the bus changed everything for him. The wall broke down into dust and there walked Taksh from the other side of the door to see his little daughter. Taksh saw her and called her Sayesha as he carefully held her to himself.

It is 2019, Taksh is playing with her daughter, Pramila has passed away a few years ago. Taksh. Isha and Aadi were all left in the Dabral family. Soon after Pramila's death, Rao succumbed to Diabetes. Isha craved to visit him for the last time but chose her ego over Rao.

Isha comes striding towards Taksh like a maniac and asks him to check his mail. She passed him the laptop, Taksh saw the starred email and smiled. Taksh was sending regular mails to the PMO for an appointment regarding the semiconductor fallback of India. It was after 6 years, a reply actually came from the other side.

After all, Taksh was the hero of the story, can we really let him be as ordinary as he is?

Snapshots

We see Taksh handed over the patent files to the secretary of the Prime Minister, greeted them, thanked them and left from there. As he walked down the lobby of the PMO, a tear of bliss rolled down from his right eye.

The patent that was the reason for his father's downfall, the patent that was his family's lifetime of achievement, he just gave it up to the people his father always protected it from and yet he walked out happy.

After the STL event, he realised it was just the credits that everyone was after and that was the reason for all that could have been avoided but now was the time, Taksh thought and decided to give up the patents to the right hands, who else it could be if not the PM himself?

Also, this was the first time Taksh met the PM in real life, previously he was just fooled by a trickery that used the name of the then PM. This time, it happened in real life and after he gave up his fathers files, he explained how in the fight for winning credits and fame, the only thing that lost was the country and he didn't want it to happen anymore.

Taksh saw how it was decades and India was still suffering because everybody was after the credits of Samrish and without that patent, they cannot recreate the technology. The only thing that suffered because of so much complications and the game of internal conflicts was — INDIA. Taksh was not okay with his country suffering because someone was trying to get credits for something he didn't do. Taksh didn't desire the credits for it anymore, he never desired it anyway but if knew the main motive of people, India may have seen the dawn of Semiconductors, earlier.

He submitted the papers and walked out victorious; walked out a HERO.

A Note Of Gratitude

Thank you for embarking on this journey with me; your choice to read my novel not only inspires a debutant like me, but ignites a passion for storytelling that seeks to unveil the hidden truths and extraordinary heroism woven within the fabric of our beloved India.